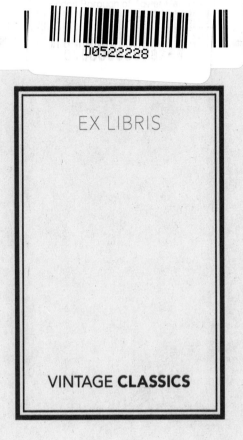

EX LIBRIS

VINTAGE CLASSICS

FLAUBERT'S PARROT

Julian Barnes is the author of ten novels, including *Metroland*, *A History of the World in 10½ Chapters* and *Arthur & George*; two books of short stories, *Cross Channel* and *The Lemon Table*; and three collections of journalism, *Letters from London*, *Something to Declare* and *The Pedant in the Kitchen*. His most recent book, *Nothing to be Frightened of*, was published in 2008. His work has been translated into more than thirty languages. In France he is the only writer to have won both the Prix Médicis (for *Flaubert's Parrot*) and the Prix Femina (for *Talking it Over*). In 1993 he was awarded the Shakespeare Prize by the FVS Foundation of Hamburg. He lives in London.

ALSO BY JULIAN BARNES

Fiction

Metroland

Before She Met Me

Staring at the Sun

A History of the World in 10½ Chapters

Talking it Over

The Porcupine

Cross Channel

England, England

Love, etc

The Lemon Table

Arthur & George

Non-fiction

Letters from London 1990–1995

Something to Declare

The Pedant in the Kitchen

Nothing to be Frightened of

Translation

In the Land of Pain

by Alphonse Daudet

JULIAN BARNES

Flaubert's Parrot

VINTAGE BOOKS
London

Published by Vintage 2009

12

'Flaubert's Parrot' was first published in the *London Review of
Books*, and 'Emma Bovary's Eyes' first appeared, in an edited form,
in *Granta*.

First published in Great Britain in 1984 by Jonathan Cape

Vintage
Random House, 20 Vauxhall Bridge Road,
London, SW1V 2SA

www.vintage-classics.info

Addresses for companies within The Random House Group Limited
can be found at: www.randomhouse.co.uk/offices.htm

The Random House Group Limited Reg. No. 954009

A CIP catalogue record for this book
is available from the British Library

ISBN 9780099540588

Penguin Random House is committed to a sustainable future for
our business, our readers and our planet. This book is made from
Forest Stewardship Council® certified paper.

Printed and bound in Great Britain by Clays Ltd, Elcograf S.p.A.

To Pat

When you write the biography of a friend,
you must do it as if you were taking *revenge* for him.

Flaubert, letter to Ernest Feydeau, 1872

Note

I am grateful to James Fenton and the Salamander Press for permission to reprint the lines from 'A German Requiem' on page 115. The translations in this book are by Geoffrey Braithwaite; though he would have been lost without the impeccable example of Francis Steegmuller.

J.B.

Contents

I

Flaubert's Parrot

Six North Africans were playing boule beneath Flaubert's statue. Clean cracks sounded over the grumble of jammed traffic. With a final, ironic caress from the fingertips, a brown hand dispatched a silver globe. It landed, hopped heavily, and curved in a slow scatter of hard dust. The thrower remained a stylish, temporary statue: knees not quite unbent, and the right hand ecstatically spread. I noticed a furled white shirt, a bare forearm and a blob on the back of the wrist. Not a watch, as I first thought, or a tattoo, but a coloured transfer: the face of a political sage much admired in the desert.

Let me start with the statue: the one above, the permanent, unstylish one, the one crying cupreous tears, the floppy-tied, square-waistcoated, baggy-trousered, straggle-moustached, wary, aloof bequeathed image of the man. Flaubert doesn't return the gaze. He stares south from the place des Carmes towards the Cathedral, out over the city he despised, and which in turn has largely ignored him. The head is defensively high: only the pigeons can see the full extent of the writer's baldness.

This statue isn't the original one. The Germans took the first Flaubert away in 1941, along with the railings and door-knockers. Perhaps he was processed into cap-badges. For a decade or so, the pedestal was empty. Then a Mayor of Rouen who was keen on statues rediscovered the original plaster cast — made by a Russian called Leopold Bernstamm — and the city council approved the making of a new image. Rouen bought itself a proper metal statue in 93 per cent copper and 7 per cent tin: the founders, Rudier of Châtillon-sous-Bagneux, assert that such an alloy is guarantee against corrosion. Two other towns, Trouville and Barentin, contributed to the project and received stone statues. These have worn less well. At Trouville Flaubert's upper thigh has had to be patched, and bits of his moustache have fallen off: structural wires poke out like twigs from a concrete stub on his upper lip.

Perhaps the foundry's assurances can be believed; perhaps this second-impression statue will last. But I see no particular grounds for confidence. Nothing much else to do with Flaubert has ever lasted. He died little more than a hundred years ago, and all that remains of him is paper. Paper, ideas, phrases, metaphors, structured prose which turns into sound. This, as it happens, is precisely what he would have wanted; it's only his admirers who sentimentally complain. The writer's house at Croisset was knocked down shortly after his death and replaced by a factory for extracting alcohol from damaged wheat. It wouldn't take much to get rid of his effigy either: if one statue-loving Mayor can put it up, another — perhaps a bookish party-liner who has half-read Sartre on Flaubert — might zealously take it down.

I begin with the statue, because that's where I began the whole project. Why does the writing make us chase the writer? Why can't we leave well alone? Why aren't the books enough? Flaubert wanted them to be: few writers believed more in the objectivity of the written text and the insignificance of the writer's personality; yet still we disobediently pursue. The image, the face, the signature; the 93 per cent copper statue and the Nadar photograph; the scrap of clothing and the lock of hair. What makes us randy for relics? Don't we believe the words enough? Do we think the leavings of a life contain some ancillary truth? When Robert Louis Stevenson died, his business-minded Scottish nanny quietly began selling hair which she claimed to have cut from the writer's head forty years earlier. The believers, the seekers, the pursuers bought enough of it to stuff a sofa.

I decided to save Croisset until later. I had five days in Rouen, and childhood instinct still makes me keep the best until last. Does the same impulse sometimes operate with writers? Hold off, hold off, the best is yet to come? If so, then how tantalising are the unfinished books. A pair of them come at once to mind: *Bouvard et Pécuchet*, where Flaubert sought to enclose and subdue the whole world, the whole of human striving and human failing; and *L'Idiot de la famille*, where Sartre sought to enclose the whole of Flaubert: enclose and subdue the master writer, the master bourgeois, the terror, the enemy, the sage. A stroke terminated the first project; blindness abbreviated the second.

I thought of writing books myself once. I had the ideas; I even made notes. But I was a doctor, married with children. You can only do one thing well: Flaubert knew that. Being a doctor was what I did well. My wife . . . died. My children are scattered now; they write whenever guilt impels. They have their own lives, naturally. 'Life! Life! To have erections!' I was reading that Flaubertian exclamation the other day. It made me feel like a stone statue with a patched upper thigh.

The unwritten books? They aren't a cause for resentment. There are too many books already. Besides, I remember the end of *L'Education sentimentale*. Frédéric and his companion Deslauriers are looking back over their lives. Their final, favourite memory is of a visit to a brothel years before, when they were still schoolboys. They had planned the trip in detail, had their hair specially curled for the occasion, and had even stolen flowers for the girls. But when they got to the brothel, Frédéric lost his nerve, and they both ran away. Such was the best day of their lives. Isn't the most reliable form of pleasure, Flaubert implies, the pleasure of anticipation? Who needs to burst into fulfilment's desolate attic?

I spent my first day wandering about Rouen, trying to recognise parts of it from when I'd come through in 1944. Large areas were bombed and shelled, of course; after forty years they're still patching up the Cathedral. I didn't find much to colour in the monochrome memories. Next day I drove west to Caen and then north to the beaches. You follow a series of weathered tin signs, erected by the

Ministère des Travaux Publics et des Transports. This way for the Circuit des Plages de Débarquement: a tourist route of the landings. East of Arromanches lie the British and Canadian beaches – Gold, Juno, Sword. Not an imaginative choice of words; so much less memorable than Omaha and Utah. Unless, of course, it's the actions that make the words memorable, and not the other way round.

Graye-sur-Mer, Courseulles-sur-Mer, Ver-sur-Mer, Asnelles, Arromanches. Down tiny sidestreets you suddenly come across a place des Royal Engineers or a place W. Churchill. Rusting tanks stand guard over beach huts; slab monuments like ships' funnels announce in English and French: 'Here on the 6th June 1944 Europe was liberated by the heroism of the Allied Forces.' It is very quiet, and not at all sinister. At Arromanches I put two one-franc pieces into the Télescope Panoramique (Très Puissant 15/60 Longue Durée) and traced the curving morse of the Mulberry Harbour far out to sea. Dot, dash, dash, dash went the concrete caissons, with the unhurried water between them. Shags had colonised these square boulders of wartime junk.

I lunched at the Hôtel de la Marine overlooking the bay. I was close to where friends had died – the sudden friends those years produced – and yet I felt unmoved. 50th Armoured Division, Second British Army. Memories came out of hiding, but not emotions; not even the memories of emotions. After lunch I went to the museum and watched a film about the landings, then drove ten kilometres to Bayeux to examine that other cross-Channel invasion of nine centuries earlier. Queen Matilda's tapestry is like horizontal cinema, the frames joined edge to edge. Both events seemed equally strange: one too distant to be true, the other too familiar to be true. How do we seize the past? Can we ever do so? When I was a medical student some pranksters at an end-of-term dance released into the hall a piglet which had been smeared with grease. It squirmed between legs, evaded capture, squealed a lot. People fell over trying to grasp it, and were made to look ridiculous in the process. The past often seems to behave like that piglet.

On my third day in Rouen I walked to the Hôtel-Dieu, the hospital where Gustave's father had been head surgeon, and where the writer spent his childhood. Along the avenue Gustave Flaubert, past the Imprimerie Flaubert and a snack-bar called Le Flaubert: you certainly feel you're going in the right direction. Parked near the hospital was a large white Peugeot hatchback: it was painted with blue stars, a telephone number and the words AMBULANCE FLAUBERT. The writer as healer? Unlikely. I remembered George Sand's matronly rebuke to her younger colleague. 'You produce desolation,' she wrote, 'and I produce consolation.' The Peugeot should have read AMBULANCE GEORGE SAND.

At the Hôtel-Dieu I was admitted by a gaunt, fidgety *gardien* whose white coat puzzled me. He wasn't a doctor, a *pharmacien* or a cricket umpire. White coats imply antisepsis and clean judgment. Why should a museum caretaker wear one — to protect Gustave's childhood from germs? He explained that the museum was devoted partly to Flaubert and partly to medical history, then hurried me round, locking the doors behind us with noisy efficiency. I was shown the room where Gustave was born, his eau-de-Cologne pot, tobacco jar and first magazine article. Various images of the writer confirmed the dire early shift he underwent from handsome youth to paunchy, balding burgher. Syphilis, some conclude. Normal nineteenth-century ageing, others reply. Perhaps it was merely that his body had a sense of decorum: when the mind inside declared itself prematurely old, the flesh did its best to conform. I kept reminding myself that he had fair hair. It's hard to remember: photographs make everyone seem dark.

The other rooms contained medical instruments of the eighteenth and nineteenth centuries: heavy metal relics coming to sharp points, and enema pumps of a calibre which surprised even me. Medicine then must have been such an exciting, desperate, violent business; nowadays it is all pills and bureaucracy. Or is it just that the past seems to contain more local colour than the present? I studied the doctoral thesis of Gustave's brother Achille: it was called 'Some Considerations on the Moment of Operation on the Strangulated Hernia'. A fraternal parallel: Achille's thesis later became Gustave's metaphor. 'I feel, against the stupidity of my time, floods of hatred which choke me. Shit rises to my mouth as in the case of a strangulated hernia. But I want to keep it, fix it, harden it; I want to concoct a paste with which I shall cover the nineteenth century, in the same way as they paint Indian pagodas with cow dung.'

The conjunction of these two museums seemed odd at first. It made sense when I remembered Lemot's famous cartoon of Flaubert dissecting Emma Bovary. It shows the novelist flourishing on the end of a large fork the dripping heart he has triumphantly torn from his heroine's body. He brandishes the organ aloft like a prize surgical exhibit, while on the left of the drawing the feet of the recumbent, violated Emma are just visible. The writer as butcher, the writer as sensitive brute.

Then I saw the parrot. It sat in a small alcove, bright green and perky-eyed, with its head at an inquiring angle. '*Psittacus*,' ran the inscription on the end of its perch: 'Parrot borrowed by G. Flaubert from the Museum of Rouen and placed on his work-table during the writing of *Un cœur simple*, where it is called Loulou, the parrot of Félicité, the principal character in the tale.' A Xeroxed letter from Flaubert confirmed the fact: the parrot, he wrote, had been on his desk for three weeks, and the sight of it was beginning to irritate him.

Loulou was in fine condition, the feathers as crisp and the eye as irritating as they must have been a hundred years earlier. I gazed at the bird, and to my surprise felt ardently in touch with this writer who disdainfully forbade posterity to take any personal interest in him. His statue was a retread; his house had been knocked down; his books naturally had their own life — responses to them weren't responses to him. But here, in this unexceptional green parrot, preserved in a routine yet mysterious fashion, was something which made me feel I had almost known the writer. I was both moved and cheered.

On the way back to my hotel I bought a student text of *Un cœur simple*. Perhaps you know the story. It's about a poor, uneducated servant-woman called Félicité, who serves the same mistress for half a century, unresentfully sacrificing her own life to those of others. She becomes attached, in turn, to a rough fiancé, to her mistress's children, to her nephew, and to an old man with a cancerous arm. All of them are casually taken from her: they die, or depart, or simply forget her. It is an existence in which, not surprisingly, the consolations of religion come to make up for the desolations of life.

The final object in Félicité's ever-diminishing chain of attachments is Loulou, the parrot. When, in due course, he too dies, Félicité has him stuffed. She keeps the adored relic beside her, and even takes to saying her prayers while kneeling before him. A doctrinal confusion develops in her simple mind: she wonders whether the Holy Ghost, conventionally represented as a dove, would not be better portrayed as a parrot. Logic is certainly on her side: parrots and Holy Ghosts can speak, whereas doves cannot. At the end of the story, Félicité herself dies. 'There was a smile on her lips. The movements of her heart slowed down beat by beat, each time more distant, like a fountain running dry or an echo disappearing; and as she breathed her final breath she thought she saw, as the heavens opened for her, a gigantic parrot hovering above her head.'

The control of tone is vital. Imagine the technical difficulty of writing a story in which a badly-stuffed bird with a ridiculous name ends up standing in for one third of the Trinity, and in which the intention is neither satirical, sentimental, nor blasphemous. Imagine further telling such a story from the point of view of an ignorant old woman without making it sound derogatory or coy. But then the aim of *Un cœur simple* is quite elsewhere: the parrot is a perfect and controlled example of the Flaubertian grotesque.

We can, if we wish (and if we disobey Flaubert), submit the bird to additional interpretation. For instance, there are submerged parallels between the life of the prematurely aged novelist and the maturely aged Félicité. Critics have sent in the ferrets. Both of them were solitary; both of them had lives stained with loss; both of them, though full of grief, were persevering. Those keen to push things further suggest that the incident in which Félicité is struck down by a mail-coach on the road to Honfleur is a submerged reference to Gustave's first epileptic fit, when he was struck down on the road outside Bourg-Achard. I don't know. How submerged does a reference have to be before it drowns?

In one cardinal way, of course, Félicité is the complete opposite of

Flaubert: she is virtually inarticulate. But you could argue that this is where Loulou comes in. The parrot, the articulate beast, a rare creature that makes human sounds. Not for nothing does Félicité confuse Loulou with the Holy Ghost, the giver of tongues.

Félicité + Loulou = Flaubert? Not exactly; but you could claim that he is present in both of them. Félicité encloses his character; Loulou encloses his voice. You could say that the parrot, representing clever vocalisation without much brain power, was Pure Word. If you were a French academic, you might say that he was *un symbole de Logos*. Being English, I hasten back to the corporeal: to that svelte, perky creature I had seen at the Hôtel-Dieu. I imagined Loulou sitting on the other side of Flaubert's desk and staring back at him like some taunting reflection from a funfair mirror. No wonder three weeks of its parodic presence caused irritation. Is the writer much more than a sophisticated parrot?

We should perhaps note at this point the four principal encounters between the novelist and a member of the parrot family. In the 1830s, during their annual holiday at Trouville, the Flaubert household regularly used to visit a retired sea-captain called Pierre Barbey; his ménage, we are told, included a magnificent parrot. In 1845 Gustave was travelling through Antibes, on his way to Italy, when he came across a sick parakeet which merited an entry in his diary; the bird used to perch carefully on the mudguard of its owner's light cart, and at dinnertime would be brought in and placed on the mantelpiece. The diarist notes the 'strange love' clearly evident between man and pet. In 1851, returning from the Orient via Venice, Flaubert heard a parrot in a gilt cage calling out over the Grand Canal its imitation of a gondolier: '*Fà eh, capo die.*' In 1853 he was again in Trouville; lodging with a *pharmacien*, he found himself constantly irritated by a parrot which screamed, '*As-tu déjeuné, Jako?*' and '*Cocu, mon petit coco.*' It also whistled '*J'ai du bon tabac.*' Was any of these four birds, in whole or in part, the inspiration behind Loulou? And did Flaubert see another living parrot between 1853 and 1876, when he borrowed a stuffed one from the Museum of Rouen? I leave such matters to the professionals.

I sat on my hotel bed; from a neighbouring room a telephone

imitated the cry of other telephones. I thought about the parrot in its alcove barely half a mile away. A cheeky bird, inducing affection, even reverence. What had Flaubert done with it after finishing *Un cœur simple*? Did he put it away in a cupboard and forget about its irritating existence until he was searching for an extra blanket? And what happened, four years later, when an apoplectic stroke left him dying on his sofa? Did he perhaps imagine, hovering above him, a gigantic parrot — this time not a welcome from the Holy Ghost but a farewell from the Word?

'I am bothered by my tendency to metaphor, decidedly excessive. I am devoured by comparisons as one is by lice, and I spend my time doing nothing but squashing them.' Words came easily to Flaubert; but he also saw the underlying inadequacy of the Word. Remember his sad definition from *Madame Bovary*: 'Language is like a cracked kettle on which we beat out tunes for bears to dance to, while all the time we long to move the stars to pity.' So you can take the novelist either way: as a pertinacious and finished stylist; or as one who considered language tragically insufficient. Sartreans prefer the second option: for them Loulou's inability to do more than repeat at second hand the phrases he hears is an indirect confession of the novelist's own failure. The parrot/writer feebly accepts language as something received, imitative and inert. Sartre himself rebuked Flaubert for passivity, for belief (or collusion in the belief) that *on est parlé* — one is spoken.

Did that burst of bubbles announce the gurgling death of another submerged reference? The point at which you suspect too much is being read into a story is when you feel most vulnerable, isolated, and perhaps stupid. Is a critic wrong to read Loulou as a symbol of the Word? Is a reader wrong — worse, sentimental — to think of that parrot at the Hôtel-Dieu as an emblem of the writer's voice? That's what I did. Perhaps this makes me as simple-minded as Félicité.

But whether you call it a tale or a text, *Un cœur simple* echoes on in the brain. Allow me to cite David Hockney, benign if unspecific, in his autobiography: 'The story really affected me, and I felt it was a subject I could get into and really use.' In 1974 Mr Hockney produced a pair of etchings: a burlesque version of Félicité's view of

Abroad (a monkey stealing away with a woman over its shoulder), and a tranquil scene of Félicité asleep with Loulou. Perhaps he will do some more in due course.

On my last day in Rouen I drove out to Croisset. Normandy rain was falling, soft and dense. What was formerly a remote village on the banks of the Seine, backdropped by green hills, has now become engulfed by thumping dockland. Pile-drivers echo; gantries hang over you, and the river is thickly commercial. Passing lorries rattle the windows of the inevitable Bar le Flaubert.

Gustave noted and approved the Oriental habit of knocking down the houses of the dead; so perhaps he would have been less hurt than his readers, his pursuers, by the destruction of his own house. The factory for extracting alcohol from damaged wheat was pulled down in its turn; and on the site there now stands, more appropriately, a large paper-mill. All that remains of Flaubert's residence is a small one-storey pavilion a few hundred yards down the road: a summer house to which the writer would retire when needing even more solitude than usual. It now looks shabby and pointless, but at least it's something. On the terrace outside, a stump of fluted column, dug up at Carthage, has been erected to commemorate the author of *Salammbô*. I pushed the gate; an Alsatian began barking, and a white-haired *gardienne* approached. No white coat for her, but a well-cut blue uniform. As I cranked up my French I remembered the trademark of the Carthaginian interpreters in *Salammbô*: each, as a symbol of his profession, has a parrot tattooed on his chest. Today the brown wrist of the African boule-player wears a Mao transfer.

The pavilion contains a single room, square with a tented ceiling. I was reminded of Félicité's room: 'It had the simultaneous air of a chapel and a bazaar.' Here too were the ironic conjunctions — trivial knick-knack beside solemn relic — of the Flaubertian grotesque. The items on display were so poorly arranged that I frequently had to get down on my knees to squint into the cabinets: the posture of the devout, but also of the junk-shop treasure-hunter.

Félicité found consolation in her assembly of stray objects, united only by their owner's affection. Flaubert did the same, preserving trivia fragrant with memories. Years after his mother's death he would still sometimes ask for her old shawl and hat, then sit down with them to dream a little. The visitor to the Croisset pavilion can almost do the same: the exhibits, carelessly laid out, catch your heart at random. Portraits, photographs, a clay bust; pipes, a tobacco jar, a letter opener; a toad-inkwell with a gaping mouth; the gold Buddha which stood on the writer's desk and never irritated him; a lock of hair, blonder, naturally, than in the photographs.

Two exhibits in a side cabinet are easy to miss: a small tumbler from which Flaubert took his last drink of water a few moments before he died; and a crumpled pad of white handkerchief with which he mopped his brow in perhaps the last gesture of his life. Such ordinary props, which seemed to forbid wailing and melodrama, made me feel I had been present at the death of a friend. I was almost embarrassed: three days before I had stood unmoved on a beach where close companions had been killed. Perhaps this is the advantage of making friends with those already dead: your feelings towards them never cool.

Then I saw it. Crouched on top of a high cupboard was another parrot. Also bright green. Also, according to both the *gardienne* and the label on its perch, the very parrot which Flaubert had borrowed from the Museum of Rouen for the writing of *Un cœur simple*. I asked permission to take the second Loulou down, set him carefully on the corner of a display cabinet, and removed his glass dome.

How do you compare two parrots, one already idealised by memory and metaphor, the other a squawking intruder? My initial response was that the second seemed less authentic than the first, mainly because it had a more benign air. The head was set straighter on the body, and its expression was less irritating than that of the bird at the Hôtel-Dieu. Then I realised the fallacy in this: Flaubert, after all, hadn't been given a choice of parrots; and even this second one, which looked the calmer company, might well get on your nerves after a couple of weeks.

I mentioned the question of authenticity to the *gardienne*. She was, understandably, on the side of her own parrot, and confidently discounted the claims of the Hôtel-Dieu. I wondered if somebody knew the answer. I wondered if it mattered to anyone except me, who had rashly invested significance in the first parrot. The writer's voice — what makes you think it can be located that easily? Such was the rebuke offered by the second parrot. As I stood looking at the possibly inauthentic Loulou, the sun lit up that corner of the room and turned his plumage more sharply yellow. I replaced the bird and thought: I am now older than Flaubert ever was. It seemed a presumptuous thing to be; sad and unmerited.

Is it ever the right time to die? It wasn't for Flaubert; or for George Sand, who didn't live to read *Un cœur simple*. 'I had begun it solely on account of her, only to please her. She died while I was in the midst of this work. So it is with all our dreams.' Is it better not to have the dreams, the work, and then the desolation of uncompleted work? Perhaps, like Frédéric and Deslauriers, we should prefer the consolation of non-fulfilment: the planned visit to the brothel, the pleasure of anticipation, and then, years later, not the memory of deeds but the memory of past anticipations? Wouldn't that keep it all cleaner and less painful?

After I got home the duplicate parrots continued to flutter in my mind: one of them amiable and straightforward, the other cocky and interrogatory. I wrote letters to various academics who might know if either of the parrots had been properly authenticated. I wrote to the French Embassy and to the editor of the Michelin guide-books. I also wrote to Mr Hockney. I told him about my trip and asked if he'd ever been to Rouen; I wondered if he'd had one or other of the parrots in mind when etching his portrait of the sleeping Félicité. If not, then perhaps he in his turn had borrowed a parrot from a museum and used it as a model. I warned him of the dangerous tendency in this species to posthumous parthenogenesis.

I hoped to get my replies quite soon.

2

Chronology

I

1821   Birth of Gustave Flaubert, second son of Achille-Cléophas Flaubert, head surgeon at the Hôtel-Dieu, Rouen, and of Anne-Justine-Caroline Flaubert, née Fleuriot. The family belongs to the successful professional middle class, and owns several properties in the vicinity of Rouen. A stable, enlightened, encouraging and normally ambitious background.

1825   Entry into service with the Flaubert family of Julie, Gustave's nurse, who remains with them until the writer's death fifty-five years later. Few servant problems will trouble his life.

c.1830   Meets Ernest Chevalier, his first close friend. A succession of intense, loyal and fertile friendships will sustain Flaubert throughout his life: of particular note are those with Alfred le Poittevin, Maxime du Camp, Louis Bouilhet and George Sand. Gustave inspires friendship easily, and fosters it with a teasing, affectionate manner.

1831–2 Enters the Collège de Rouen and proves an impressive student, strong in history and literature. His earliest piece of writing to come down to us, an essay on Corneille, dates from 1832. Throughout his adolescence he composes abundantly, both drama and fiction.

1836 Meets Elisa Schlesinger, wife of a German music publisher, in Trouville and conceives an 'enormous' passion for her. This passion illuminates the rest of his adolescence. She treats him with great kindness and affection; they remain in touch for the next forty years. Looking back, he is relieved she didn't return his passion: 'Happiness is like the pox. Catch it too soon, and it wrecks your constitution.'

c.1836 Gustave's sexual initiation with one of his mother's maids. This is the start of an active and colourful erotic career, veering from brothel to salon, from Cairo bath-house boy to Parisian poetess. In early manhood he is extremely attractive to women and his speed of sexual recuperation is, by his own account, very impressive; but even in later life his courtly manner, intelligence and fame ensure that he is not unattended.

1837 His first published work appears in the Rouen magazine *Le Colibri*.

1840 Passes his *baccalauréat*. Travels to the Pyrenees with a family friend, Dr Jules Cloquet. Though often considered an unbudgeable hermit, Flaubert in fact travels extensively: to Italy and Switzerland (1845), Brittany (1847), Egypt, Palestine, Syria, Turkey, Greece and Italy (1849–51), England (1851, 1865, 1866, 1871), Algeria and Tunisia (1858), Germany (1865), Belgium (1871) and Switzerland (1874). Compare the case of his *alter ego* Louis Bouilhet, who dreamed of China and never got to England.

1843   As a law student in Paris, he meets Victor Hugo.

1844   Gustave's first epileptic attack puts an end to his legal studies in Paris and confines him to the new family house at Croisset. Abandoning the law, however, causes little pain, and since his confinement brings both the solitude and the stable base needed for a life of writing, the attack proves beneficial in the long run.

1846   Meets Louise Colet, 'the Muse', and begins his most celebrated affair: a prolonged, passionate, fighting two-parter (1846–8, 1851–4). Though ill-matched in temperament and incompatible in aesthetics, Gustave and Louise nevertheless last together far longer than most would have predicted. Should we regret the end of their affair? Only because it means the end of Gustave's resplendent letters to her.

1851–7 The writing, publication, trial and triumphant acquittal of *Madame Bovary*. A *succès de scandale*, praised by authors as diverse as Lamartine, Sainte-Beuve and Baudelaire. In 1846, doubting his ability ever to write anything worth publishing, Gustave had announced, 'If I do make an appearance, one day, it will be in full armour.' Now his breastplate dazzles and his lance is everywhere. The curé of Canteleu, the next village to Croisset, forbids his parishioners to read the novel. After 1857, literary success leads naturally to social success: Flaubert is seen more in Paris. He meets the Goncourts, Renan, Gautier, Baudelaire and Sainte-Beuve. In 1862 the series of literary dinners at Magny's are instituted: Flaubert is a regular from December of that year.

1862   Publication of *Salammbô*. *Succès fou*. Sainte-Beuve writes to Matthew Arnold: '*Salammbô* is our great event!' The novel provides the theme for several costume balls in Paris. It even provides the name for a new brand of *petit four*.

1863   Flaubert begins to frequent the salon of Princesse Mathilde, niece of Napoleon I. The bear of Croisset eases into the pelt of the social lion. He himself receives on Sunday afternoons. The year also contains his first exchange of letters with George Sand, and his meeting with Turgenev. His friendship with the Russian novelist marks the beginning of a wider European fame.

1864   Presentation to the Emperor Napoleon III at Compiegne. The peak of Gustave's social success. He sends camellias to the Empress.

1866   Created *chevalier de la Légion d'honneur*.

1869   Publication of *L'Education sentimentale*: Flaubert always claims it as *un chef-d'œuvre*. Despite the legend of heroic struggle (which he himself initiates), writing comes easily to Flaubert. He complains a lot, but such complaints are always couched in letters of astonishing fluency. For a quarter of a century he produces one large, solid book, requiring considerable research, every five to seven years. He might agonise over the word, the phrase, the assonance, but he never endures a writer's block.

1874   Publication of *La Tentation de saint Antoine*. Despite its strangeness, a gratifying commercial success.

1877   Publication of *Trois Contes*. A critical and popular success: for the first time Flaubert receives a favourable review from *Le Figaro*; the book goes through five editions in three years. Flaubert begins work on *Bouvard et Pécuchet*. During these final years, his pre-eminence among French novelists is admitted by the next generation. He is fêted and revered. His Sunday afternoons become famous events in literary society; Henry James calls on the Master. In 1879 Gustave's friends institute the annual Saint Polycarpe dinners in his honour. In 1880 the five co-authors of *Les Soirées de Medan*, including Zola and Maupassant, present him with an inscribed copy: the gift can be seen as a symbolic salute to Realism from Naturalism.

1880   Full of honour, widely loved, and still working hard to the end, Gustave Flaubert dies at Croisset.

II

1817   Death of Caroline Flaubert (aged twenty months), the second child of Achille-Cléophas Flaubert and Anne-Justine-Caroline Flaubert.

1819   Death of Emile-Cléophas Flaubert (aged eight months), their third child.

1821   Birth of Gustave Flaubert, their fifth child.

1822   Death of Jules Alfred Flaubert (aged three years and five months), their fourth child. His brother Gustave, born *entre deux morts*, is delicate and not expected to live long. Dr Flaubert buys a family plot at the Cimetière Monumental and has a small grave dug in preparation for Gustave. Surprisingly, he survives. He proves a slow child, content to sit for hours with his finger in his mouth and an 'almost stupid' expression on his face. For Sartre, he is 'the family idiot'.

1836   The start of a hopeless, obsessive passion for Elisa Schlesinger which cauterises his heart and renders him incapable of ever fully loving another woman. Looking back, he records: 'Each of us possesses in his heart a royal chamber. I have bricked mine up.'

1839   Expelled from the Collège de Rouen for rowdyism and dis-
obedience.

1843   The Faculty of Law at Paris announces its first-year examination results. The examiners declare their views by means of
red or black balls. Gustave receives two red and two black,
and is therefore failed.

1844   Shattering first attack of epilepsy; others are to follow. 'Each
attack', Gustave writes later, 'was like a haemorrhage of the
nervous system ... It was a snatching of the soul from the
body, excruciating.' He is bled, given pills and infusions,
put on a special diet, forbidden alcohol and tobacco; a regime
of strict confinement and maternal care is necessary if he is
not to claim his place at the cemetery. Without having
entered the world, Gustave now retires from it. 'So, you are
guarded like a young girl?' Louise Colet later taunts, accurately. For all but the last eight years of his life, Mme Flaubert
watches suffocatingly over his welfare and censors his travel
plans. Gradually, over the decades, her frailty overtakes his:
by the time he has almost ceased to be a worry to her, she has
become a burden to him.

1846   Death of Gustave's father, quickly followed by that of his
beloved sister Caroline (aged twenty-one), which thrusts on
to him proxy fatherhood of his niece. Throughout his life,
he is constantly bruised by the deaths of those close to him.
And there are other ways for friends to die: in June Alfred le
Poittevin marries. Gustave feels it is his third bereavement
of the year: 'You are doing something abnormal,' he complains. To Maxime du Camp that year he writes, 'Tears are
to the heart what water is to a fish.' Is it a consolation that in
the same year he meets Louise Colet? Pedantry and recalci-
trance are mismatched with immoderation and possess-
iveness. A mere six days after she becomes his mistress, the
pattern of their relationship is set: 'Moderate your cries!' he

complains to her. 'They are torturing me. What do you want me to do? Am I to leave everything and live in Paris? Impossible.' This impossible relationship drags on nevertheless for eight years; Louise is puzzlingly unable to grasp that Gustave can love her without ever wanting to see her. 'If I were a woman,' he writes after six years, 'I wouldn't want myself for a lover. A one-night stand, yes; but an intimate relationship, no.'

1848   Death of Alfred le Poittevin, aged thirty-two. 'I see that I've never loved anyone — man or woman — as I loved him.' Twenty-five years later: 'Not a day passes that I don't think of him.'

1849   Gustave reads his first full-length adult work, *La Tentation de saint Antoine*, to his two closest friends, Bouilhet and Du Camp. The reading takes four days, at the rate of eight hours per day. After embarrassed consultation, the listeners tell him to throw it on the fire.

1850   In Egypt, Gustave catches syphilis. Much of his hair falls out; he grows stout. Mme Flaubert, meeting him in Rome the following year, scarcely recognises her son, and finds that he has become very coarse. Middle age begins here. 'Scarcely are you born before you begin rotting.' Over the years all but one of his teeth will fall out; his saliva will be permanently blackened by mercury treatment.

1851–7 *Madame Bovary*. The composition is painful — 'Writing this book I am like a man playing the piano with lead balls attached to his knuckles' — and the prosecution frightening. In later years Flaubert comes to resent the insistent fame of his masterpiece, which makes others see him as a one-book author. He tells Du Camp that if ever he had a stroke of good luck on the Bourse he would buy up 'at any cost' all copies of *Madame Bovary* in circulation: 'I should throw them into the fire, and never hear of them again.'

1862   Elisa Schlesinger is interned in a mental hospital; she is diagnosed as suffering from 'acute melancholia'. After the publication of *Salammbô*, Flaubert begins to run with rich friends. But he remains childlike in financial matters: his mother has to sell property to pay his debts. In 1867 he secretly hands over control of his financial affairs to his niece's husband, Ernest Commanville. Over the next thirteen years, through extravagance, incompetent management and bad luck, Flaubert loses all his money.

1869   Death of Louis Bouilhet, whom he had once called 'the Seltzer water which helped me digest life'. 'In losing my Bouilhet, I had lost my midwife, the man who saw more deeply into my thought than I did myself.' Death also of Sainte-Beuve. 'Another one gone! The little band is diminishing! Who is there to talk about literature with now?' Publication of *L'Education sentimentale*; a critical and commercial flop. Of the hundred and fifty complimentary copies sent to friends and acquaintances, barely thirty are even acknowledged.

1870   Death of Jules de Goncourt: only three of the seven friends who started the Magny dinners in 1862 are now left. During the Franco-Prussian war, the enemy occupies Croisset. Ashamed of being French, Flaubert stops wearing his *Légion d'honneur*, and resolves to ask Turgenev what he has to do to take Russian citizenship.

1872   Death of Mme Flaubert: 'I have realised during the last fortnight that my poor dear old mother was the person I loved the most. It's as if part of my entrails had been torn out.' Death also of Gautier. 'With him, the last of my intimate friends is gone. The list is closed.'

1874 Flaubert makes his theatrical début with *Le Candidat*. It is a complete flop; actors leave the stage with tears in their eyes. The play is taken off after four performances. Publication of *La Tentation de saint Antoine*. 'Torn to pieces,' Flaubert notes, 'by everything from the *Figaro* to the *Revue des deux mondes* . . . What comes as a surprise is the hatred underlying much of this criticism − hatred for me, for my person − deliberate denigration . . . This avalanche of abuse does depress me.'

1875 The financial ruin of Ernest Commanville drags Flaubert down too. He sells his farm at Deauville; he has to plead with his niece not to turn him out of Croisset. She and Commanville nickname him 'the consumer'. In 1879 he is reduced to accepting a state pension arranged for him by friends.

1876 Death of Louise Colet. Death of George Sand. 'My heart is becoming a necropolis.' Gustave's last years are arid and solitary. He tells his niece he regrets not having married.

1880 Impoverished, lonely and exhausted, Gustave Flaubert dies. Zola, in his obituary notice, comments that he was unknown to four-fifths of Rouen, and detested by the other fifth. He leaves *Bouvard et Pécuchet* unfinished. Some say the labour of the novel killed him; Turgenev told him before he started that it would be better as a short story. After the funeral a group of mourners, including the poets François Coppée and Théodore de Banville, have dinner in Rouen to honour the departed writer. They discover, on sitting down to table, that they are thirteen. The superstitious Banville insists that another guest be found, and Gautier's son-in-law Émile Bergerat is sent to scour the streets. After several rebuffs he returns with a private on leave. The soldier has never heard of Flaubert, but is longing to meet Coppée.

III

1842   Me and my books, in the same apartment: like a gherkin in its vinegar.

1846   When I was still quite young I had a complete presentiment of life. It was like the nauseating smell of cooking escaping from a ventilator: you don't have to have eaten it to know that it would make you throw up.

1846   I did with you what I have done before with those I loved best: I showed them the bottom of the bag, and the acrid dust that rose from it made them choke.

1846   My life is riveted to that of another [Mme Flaubert], and will be so as long as that other life endures. A piece of seaweed blowing in the wind, I am held to the rock by a single hardy thread. If it broke, where would this poor useless plant fly off to?

1846   You want to prune the tree. Its unruly branches, thick with leaves, push out in all directions to sniff the air and the sun. But you want to make me into a charming espalier, stretched against a wall, bearing fine fruit that a child could pick without even using a ladder.

1846   Don't think that I belong to that vulgar race of men who feel disgust after pleasure, and for whom love exists only as lust. No: in me, what rises doesn't subside so quickly. Moss grows on the castles of my heart as soon as they are built; but it takes some time for them to fall into ruin, if they ever completely do.

1846   I am like a cigar: you have to suck on the end to get me going.

1846   Amongst those who go to sea there are the navigators who
       discover new worlds, adding continents to the earth and
       stars to the heavens: they are the masters, the great, the
       eternally splendid. Then there are those who spit terror
       from their gun-ports, who pillage, who grow rich and fat.
       Others go off in search of gold and silk under foreign skies.
       Still others catch salmon for the gourmet or cod for the
       poor. I am the obscure and patient pearl-fisherman who
       dives into the deepest waters and comes up with empty
       hands and a blue face. Some fatal attraction draws me down
       into the abysses of thought, down into those innermost
       recesses which never cease to fascinate the strong. I shall
       spend my life gazing at the ocean of art, where others
       voyage or fight; and from time to time I'll entertain myself
       by diving for those green and yellow shells that nobody will
       want. So I shall keep them for myself and cover the walls of
       my hut with them.

1846   I am only a literary lizard basking the day away beneath the
       great sun of Beauty. That's all.

1846   Deep within me there is a radical, intimate, bitter and
       incessant *boredom* which prevents me from enjoying any-
       thing and which smothers my soul. It reappears at any
       excuse, just as the swollen corpses of drowned dogs pop to
       the surface despite the stones that have been tied round their
       necks.

1847   People are like food. There are lots of bourgeois who seem
       to me like boiled beef: all steam, no juice, and no taste (it fills
       you up straight away and is much eaten by bumpkins).
       Other people are like white meat, freshwater fish, slender
       eels from the muddy river-bed, oysters (of varying degrees
       of saltiness), calves' heads, and sugared porridge. Me? I'm
       like a runny, stinking macaroni cheese, which you have to
       eat a lot of times before you develop a taste for it. You do

finally get to like it, but only after it has made your stomach heave on countless occasions.

1847 Some people have a tender heart and a tough mind. I'm the opposite: I have a tender mind but a rough heart. I'm like a coconut which keeps its milk locked away beneath several layers of wood. You need an axe to open it, and then what do you find as often as not? A sort of sour cream.

1847 You had hoped to find in me a fire which scorched and blazed and illuminated everything; which shed a cheerful light, dried out damp wainscoting, made the air healthier and rekindled life. Alas! I'm only a poor nightlight, whose red wick splutters in a lake of bad oil full of water and bits of dust.

1851 With me, friendship is like the camel: once started, there is no way of stopping it.

1852 As you get older, the heart sheds its leaves like a tree. You cannot hold out against certain winds. Each day tears away a few more leaves; and then there are the storms which break off several branches at one go. And while nature's greenery grows back again in the spring, that of the heart never grows back.

1852 What an awful thing life is, isn't it? It's like soup with lots of hairs floating on the surface. You have to eat it nevertheless.

1852 I laugh at everything, even at that which I love the most. There is no fact, thing, feeling or person over which I have not blithely run my clownishness, like an iron roller imparting sheen to cloth.

1852 I love my work with a frantic and perverted love, as an ascetic loves the hair-shirt which scratches his belly.

34

1852 All of us Normans have a little cider in our veins: it's a bitter, fermented drink which sometimes bursts the bung.

1853 As for this business of my moving at once to Paris, we'll have to put it off, or rather settle it here and now. This is *impossible* for me now . . . I know myself well enough, and it would mean losing a whole winter, and perhaps the whole book. Bouilhet can talk: he's happy writing anywhere; he's been working away for a dozen years despite continual disturbances . . . But I am like a row of milk-pans: if you want the cream to form, you have to leave them exactly where they are.

1853 I'm dazzled by your facility. In ten days you'll have written six stories! I don't understand it . . . I'm like one of those old aqueducts: there's so much rubbish clogging up the banks of my thought that it flows slowly, and only spills from the end of my pen drop by drop.

1854 I pigeon-hole my life, and keep everything in its place; I'm as full of drawers and compartments as an old travelling trunk, all roped up and fastened with three big leather straps.

1854 You ask for love, you complain that I don't send you flowers? Flowers, indeed! If that's what you want, find yourself some wet-eared boy stuffed with fine manners and all the right ideas. I'm like the tiger, which has bristles of hair at the end of its cock, with which it lacerates the female.

1857 Books aren't made in the way that babies are: they are made like pyramids. There's some long-pondered plan, and then great blocks of stone are placed one on top of the other, and it's back-breaking, sweaty, time-consuming work. And all to no purpose! It just stands like that in the desert! But it towers over it prodigiously. Jackals piss at the base of it, and

35

bourgeois clamber to the top of it, etc. Continue this comparison.

1857   There is a Latin phrase which means roughly, 'To pick up a farthing from the shit with your teeth.' It was a rhetorical figure applied to the miserly. I am like them: I will stop at nothing to find gold.

1867   It's true that many things infuriate me. The day I stop being indignant I shall fall flat on my face, like a doll when you take away its prop.

1872   My heart remains intact, but my feelings are sharpened on the one hand and dulled on the other, like an old knife that has been too often sharpened, which has notches, and breaks easily.

1872   Never have things of the spirit counted for so little. Never has hatred for everything great been so manifest − disdain for Beauty, execration of literature. I have always tried to live in an ivory tower, but a tide of shit is beating at its walls, threatening to undermine it.

1873   I still carry on turning out my sentences, like a bourgeois turning out napkin rings on a lathe in his attic. It gives me something to do, and it affords me some private pleasure.

1875   Despite your advice, I can't manage to 'harden myself' ... My sensitivities are all aquiver − my nerves and my brain are sick, very sick; I feel them to be so. But there I go, complaining again, and I don't want to distress you. I'll confine myself to your mention of a 'rock'. Know, then, that very old granite sometimes turns into layers of clay.

1875   I feel uprooted, like a mass of dead seaweed tossed here and there in the waves.

1880   When will the book be finished? That's the question. If it is
to appear next winter, I haven't a minute to lose between
now and then. But there are moments when I'm so tired that
I feel I'm liquefying like an old Camembert.

3

Finders Keepers

You can define a net in one of two ways, depending on your point of view. Normally, you would say that it is a meshed instrument designed to catch fish. But you could, with no great injury to logic, reverse the image and define a net as a jocular lexicographer once did: he called it a collection of holes tied together with string.

You can do the same with a biography. The trawling net fills, then the biographer hauls it in, sorts, throws back, stores, fillets and sells. Yet consider what he doesn't catch: there is always far more of that. The biography stands, fat and worthy-burgherish on the shelf, boastful and sedate: a shilling life will give you all the facts, a ten pound one all the hypotheses as well. But think of everything that got away, that fled with the last deathbed exhalation of the biographee. What chance would the craftiest biographer stand against the subject who saw him coming and decided to amuse himself?

I first met Ed Winterton when he put his hand on mine in the Europa Hotel. Just my little joke; though true as well. It was at a provincial booksellers' fair and I had reached a little more quickly than he for the same copy of Turgenev's *Literary Reminiscences*. The conjunction induced immediate apologies, as embarrassed on his side as they were on mine. When we each realised that bibliophilic lust was the only emotion which had produced this laying on of hands, Ed murmured,

'Step outside and let's discuss it.'

Over an indifferent pot of tea we revealed our separate paths to the same book. I explained about Flaubert; he announced his interest in Gosse and in English literary society towards the end of the last century. I meet few American academics, and was pleasantly surprised that this one was bored by Bloomsbury, and happy to leave the modern movement to his younger and more ambitious colleagues. But then Ed Winterton liked to present himself as a failure. He was in his early forties, balding, with a pinky glabrous complexion and square rimless spectacles: the banker type of academic, circumspect and moral. He bought English clothes without looking at all English. He remained the sort of American who always wears a mackintosh in London because he knows that in this city rain falls out of a clear sky. He was even wearing his mackintosh in the lounge of the Europa Hotel.

His air of failure had nothing desperate about it; rather, it seemed to stem from an unresented realisation that he was not cut out for success, and his duty was therefore to ensure only that he failed in a correct and acceptable fashion. At one point, when discussing the improbability of his Gosse biography ever being finished, let alone published, he paused and dropped his voice:

'But in any case I sometimes wonder if Mr Gosse would have approved of what I'm doing.'

'You mean ... ' I knew little of Gosse, and my widened eyes hinted perhaps too clearly at naked laundresses, illegitimate half-castes and dismembered bodies.

'Oh no, no, no. Just the thought of *writing* about him. He might think it was a bit of a ... low blow.'

I let him have the Turgenev, of course, if only to escape a discussion about the morality of possession. I didn't see where ethics came into the ownership of a second-hand book; but Ed did. He promised to be in touch if ever he ran down another copy. Then we briefly discussed the rights and wrongs of my paying for his tea.

I didn't expect to hear from him again, let alone on the subject which provoked his letter to me about a year later. 'Are you interested at all in Juliet Herbert? It sounds a fascinating relationship, judging by the material. I'll be in London in August, if you will. Ever, Ed (Winterton).'

What does the fiancée feel when she snaps open the box and sees the ring set in purple velvet? I never asked my wife; and it's too late now. Or what did Flaubert feel as he waited for the dawn on top of the Great Pyramid and finally saw that crack of gold shine from the purple velvet of the night? Astonishment, awe and a fierce glee came into my heart as I read those two words in Ed's letter. No, not 'Juliet Herbert', the other two: first 'fascinating' and then 'material'. And beyond glee, beyond hard work as well, was there something else? A shameful thought of an honorary degree somewhere?

Juliet Herbert is a great hole tied together with string. She became governess to Flaubert's niece Caroline at some time in the mid-1850s, and remained at Croisset for a few undetermined years; then she returned to London. Flaubert wrote to her, and she to him; they visited one another every so often. Beyond this, we know nothing. Not a single letter to or from her has survived. We know almost nothing about her family. We do not even know what she looked like. No description of her survives, and none of Flaubert's friends thought to mention her after his death, when most other women of importance in his life were being memorialised.

Biographers disagree about Juliet Herbert. For some, the shortage of evidence indicates that she was of small significance in Flaubert's life; others conclude from this absence precisely the opposite, and assert that the tantalising governess was certainly one of the writer's mistresses, possibly the Great Unknown Passion of his life, and perhaps even his fiancée. Hypothesis is spun directly from the temperament of the biographer. Can we deduce love for Juliet Herbert from the fact that Gustave called his greyhound Julio? Some can. It seems a little tendentious to me. And if we do, what do we then deduce from the fact that in various letters Gustave addresses his niece as 'Loulou', the name he later transfers to Félicité's parrot? Or from the fact that George Sand had a ram called Gustave?

Flaubert's one overt reference to Juliet Herbert comes in a letter to Bouilhet, written after the latter had visited Croisset:

Since I saw you excited by the governess, I too have become excited. At table, my eyes willingly followed the gentle slope of her breast. I believe she notices this for, five or six times per meal, she looks as if she had caught the sun. What a pretty comparison one could make between the slope of the breast and the glacis of a fortress. The cupids tumble about on it, as they storm the citadel. (To be said in our Sheikh's voice) 'Well, I certainly know what piece of artillery I'd be pointing in that direction.'

Should we jump to conclusions? Frankly, this is the kind of boastful, nudging stuff that Flaubert was always writing to his male friends. I find it unconvincing myself: true desire isn't so easily diverted into metaphor. But then, all biographers secretly want to annex and channel the sex-lives of their subjects; you must make your judgment on me as well as on Flaubert.

Had Ed really discovered some Juliet Herbert material? I admit I began feeling possessive in advance. I imagined myself presenting it in one of the more important literary journals; perhaps I might let the *TLS* have it. 'Juliet Herbert: A Mystery Solved,' by Geoffrey Braithwaite', illustrated with one of those photographs in which you can't quite read the handwriting. I also began to worry at the thought of Ed blurting out his discovery on campus and guilelessly yielding up his cache to some ambitious Gallicist with an astronaut's haircut.

But these were unworthy and, I hope, untypical feelings. Mostly, I was thrilled at the idea of discovering the secret of Gustave and Juliet's relationship (what else could the word 'fascinating' mean in Ed's letter?). I was also thrilled that the material might help me imagine even more exactly what Flaubert was like. The net was being pulled tighter. Would we find out, for instance, how the writer behaved in London?

This was of particular interest. Cultural exchange between England and France in the nineteenth century was at best pragmatic. French writers didn't cross the Channel to discuss aesthetics with their English counterparts; they were either running from prosecution or looking for a job. Hugo and Zola came over as exiles; Verlaine and Mallarmé came over as schoolmasters. Villiers de l'Isle-Adam, chronically poor yet crazily practical, came over in search of an heiress. A Parisian marriage-broker had kitted him out for the expedition with a fur overcoat, a repeating alarm watch and a new set of false teeth, all to be paid for when the writer landed the heiress's dowry. But Villiers, tirelessly accident-prone, botched the wooing. The heiress rejected him, the broker turned up to reclaim the coat and watch, and the discarded suitor was left adrift in London, full of teeth but penniless.

So what of Flaubert? We know little about his four trips to England. We know that the Great Exhibition of 1851 secured his unexpected approval — 'a very fine thing, despite being admired by everyone' — but his notes on this first visit amount to a mere seven pages: two on the British Museum, plus five on the Chinese and Indian sections at Crystal Palace. What were his first impressions of us? He must have told Juliet. Did we live up to our entries in his *Dictionnaire des idées reçues* (ENGLISHMEN: *All rich*. ENGLISHWOMEN: *Express surprise that they produce pretty children*)?

And what of subsequent visits, when he had become author of the notorious *Madame Bovary*? Did he search out English writers? Did he search out English brothels? Did he cosily stay at home with Juliet, staring at her over dinner and then storming her fortress? Were they perhaps (I half-hoped so) merely friends? Was Flaubert's English as hit-and-miss as it seems from his letters? Did he talk only Shakespearean? And did he complain much about the fog?

When I met Ed at the restaurant, he was looking even less successful than before. He told me about budget cuts, a cruel world, and his own lack of publications. I deduced, rather than heard, that he had been sacked. He explained the irony of his dismissal: it sprang from his devotion to his work, his unwillingness to do Gosse anything less than justice when presenting him to the world. Academic superiors had suggested that he cut corners. Well, he wouldn't do so. He respected writing and writers too much for that. 'I mean, don't we owe these fellers something in return?' he concluded.

Perhaps I offered slightly less than the expected sympathy. But then, can you alter the way luck flows? Just for once, it was flowing for me. I had ordered my dinner quickly, scarcely caring what I ate; Ed had pondered the menu as if he were Verlaine being bought his first square meal in months. Listening to Ed's tedious lament for himself and watching him slowly consume whitebait at the same time had used up my patience; though it had not diminished my excitement.

'Right,' I said, as we started our main course, 'Juliet Herbert.'

'Oh,' he said, 'yes.' I could see he might need prodding. 'It's an odd story.'

'It would be.'

'Yes.' Ed seemed a little pained, almost embarrassed. 'Well, I was over here about six months ago, tracking down one of Mr Gosse's distant descendants. Not that I expected to find anything. It was just that, as far as I knew, nobody had ever talked to the lady in question, and I thought it was my . . . duty to see her. Perhaps some family legend I hadn't accounted for had come down to her.'

'And?'

'And? Oh, it hadn't. No, she wasn't really of any help. It was a nice day, though. Kent.' He looked pained again; he seemed to miss the mackintosh which the waiter had ruthlessly deprived him of. 'Ah, but I see what you mean. What *had* come down to her was the letters. Now let me get this right; you'll correct me, I hope. Juliet Herbert died 1909 or so? Yes. She had a cousin, woman cousin. Yes. Now, this woman found the letters and took them to Mr Gosse, asked him his opinion of their value. Mr Gosse thought he was being touched for money, so he said they were interesting but not worth anything. Whereupon this cousin apparently just handed them over to him and said, If they're not worth anything, you take them. Which he did.'

'How do you know all this?'

'There was a letter attached in Mr Gosse's hand.'

'And so?'

'And so they came down to this lady. Kent. I'm afraid she asked me the same question. Were they worth anything? I regret I behaved in a rather immoral fashion. I told her they had been valuable when Gosse had examined them, but they weren't any more. I said they were still quite interesting, but they weren't worth much because half of them were written in French. Then I bought them off her for fifty pounds.'

'Good God.' No wonder he looked shifty.

'Yes, it was rather bad, wasn't it? I can't really excuse myself; though the fact that Mr Gosse himself had lied when obtaining them did seem to blur the issue. It raises an interesting ethical point, don't you think? The fact is, I was rather depressed at losing my job, and I thought I'd take them home and sell them and then be able to carry on with my book.'

'How many letters are there?'

'About seventy-five. Three dozen or so on each side. That's how we settled on the price – a pound apiece for the ones in English, fifty pence for the ones in French.'

'Good God.' I wondered what they might be worth. Perhaps a thousand times what he paid for them. Or more.

'Yes.'

'Well, go on, tell me about them.'

'Ah.' He paused, and gave me a look which might have been roguish if he hadn't been such a meek, pedantic fellow. Probably he was enjoying my excitement. 'Well, fire away. What do you want to know?'

'You have read them?'

'Oh yes.'

'And, and ... ' I didn't know what to ask. Ed was definitely enjoying this now. 'And – did they have an affair? They did, didn't they?'

'Oh yes, certainly.'

'And when did it start? Soon after she got to Croisset?'

'Oh yes, quite soon.'

Well, that unravelled the letter to Bouilhet: Flaubert was playing the tease, pretending he had just as much, or just as little, chance as his friend with the governess; whereas in fact ...

'And it continued all the time she was there?'

'Oh yes.'

'And when he came to England?'

44

'Yes, that too.'

'And was she his fiancée?'

'It's hard to say. Pretty nearly, I'd guess. There are some references in both their letters, mostly jocular. Remarks about the little English governess trapping the famous French man of letters; what would she do if he were imprisoned for another outrage against public morals; that sort of thing.'

'Well, well, well. And do we find out what she was like?'

'What she was like? Oh, you mean to look at?'

'Yes. There wasn't . . . there wasn't . . . ' He sensed my hope. ' . . . a photograph?'

'A photograph? Yes, several, as a matter of fact; from some Chelsea studio, printed on heavy card. He must have asked her to send him some. Is that of interest?'

'It's incredible. What did she look like?'

'Pretty nice in an unmemorable sort of way. Dark hair, strong jaw, good nose. I didn't look too closely; not really my type.'

'And did they get on well together?' I hardly knew what I wanted to ask any more. *Flaubert's English fiancée*, I was thinking to myself. By Geoffrey Braithwaite.

'Oh yes, they seemed to. They seemed very fond. He'd mastered quite a range of English endearments by the end.'

'So he could manage the language?'

'Oh yes, there are several long passages of English in his letters.'

'And did he like London?'

'He liked it. How could he not? It was his fiancée's city of residence.'

Dear old Gustave, I murmured to myself; I felt quite tender towards him. Here, in this city, a century and a few years ago, with a compatriot of mine who had captured his heart. 'Did he complain about the fog?'

'Of course. He wrote something like, How do you manage to live with such fog? By the time a gentleman has recognised a lady as she comes at him out of the fog, it is already too late to raise his hat. I'm surprised the race doesn't die out when such conditions make difficult the natural courtesies.'

45

Oh yes, that was the tone — elegant, teasing, slightly lubricious. 'And what about the Great Exhibition? Does he go into detail about that? I bet he rather liked it.'

'He did. Of course, that was a few years before they first met, but he does mention it in a sentimental fashion — wonders if he might unknowingly have passed her in the crowds. He thought it was a bit awful, but also really rather splendid. He seems to have looked at all the exhibits as if they were an enormous display of source material for him.'

'And. Hmm.' Well, why not. 'I suppose he didn't go to any brothels?'

Ed looked at me rather crossly. 'Well, he was writing to his girl-friend, wasn't he? He'd hardly be boasting about that.'

'No, of course not.' I felt chastened. I also felt exhilarated. My letters. *My* letters. Winterton was planning to let me publish them, wasn't he?

'So when can I see them? You did bring them with you?'

'Oh no.'

'You didn't?' Well, no doubt it was sensible to keep them all in a safe place. Travel has its dangers. Unless ... unless there was something I hadn't understood. Perhaps ... did he want money? I suddenly realised I knew absolutely nothing about Ed Winterton, except that he was the owner of my copy of Turgenev's *Literary Reminiscences*. 'You didn't even bring a single one with you?'

'No. You see, I burnt them.'

'You what?'

'Yes, well, that's what I mean by it being an odd story.'

'It sounds like a criminal story at the moment.'

'I was sure you'd understand,' he said, much to my surprise; then smiled broadly. 'I mean, you of all people. In fact, at first I decided not to tell anyone at all, but then I remembered you. I thought that one person in the business ought to be told. Just for the record.'

'Go on.' The man was a maniac, that much was plain. No wonder they'd kicked him out of his university. If only they'd done it years earlier.

'Well, you see, they were full of fascinating stuff, the letters. Very long, a lot of them, full of reflections about other writers, public life, and so on. They were even more unbuttoned than his normal letters. Perhaps it was because he was sending them out of the country that he allowed himself such freedom.' Did this criminal, this sham, this failure, this murderer, this bald pyromaniac know what he was doing to me? Very probably he did. 'And her letters were really quite fine in their way too. Told her whole life story. Very revealing about Flaubert. Full of nostalgic descriptions of home life at Croisset. She obviously had a very good eye. Noticed things I shouldn't think anyone else would have done.'

'Go on.' I waved grimly at the waiter. I wasn't sure I could stay there much longer. I wanted to tell Winterton how really pleased I was that the British had burnt the White House to the ground.

'No doubt you're wondering why I destroyed the letters. I can see you're kind of edgy about something. Well, in the very last communication between the two of them, he says that in the event of his death, her letters will be sent back to her, and she is to burn both sides of the correspondence.'

'Did he give any reasons?'

'No.'

This seemed strange, assuming that the maniac was telling the truth. But then Gustave did burn much of his correspondence with Du Camp. Perhaps some temporary pride in his family origins had asserted itself and he didn't want the world to know that he had nearly married an English governess. Or perhaps he didn't want us to know that his famous devotion to solitude and art had nearly been overthrown. But the world would know. I would tell it, one way or another.

'So you see, of course, I didn't have any alternative. I mean, if your business is writers, you have to behave towards them with integrity, don't you? You have to do what they say, even if other people don't.' What a smug, moralising bastard he was. He wore ethics the way tarts wear make-up. And then he managed to mix into the same expression both the earlier shiftiness and the later smugness. 'There was also something else in this last letter of his. A rather strange instruction on top of asking Miss Herbert to burn the

47

correspondence. He said, If anyone ever asks you what my letters contained, or what my life was like, please lie to them. Or rather, since I cannot ask you of all people to lie, just tell them what it is you think they want to hear.'

I felt like Villiers de l'Isle-Adam: someone had lent me a fur overcoat and a repeating watch for a few days, then cruelly snatched them back. It was lucky that the waiter returned at that point. Besides, Winterton was not as stupid as all that: he had pushed his chair well back from the table and was playing with his fingernails. 'The pity of it is,' he said, as I tucked away my credit card, 'that I probably now won't be able to finance Mr Gosse. But I'm sure you'll agree it's been an interesting moral decision.'

I think the remark I then made was deeply unfair to Mr Gosse both as a writer and as a sexual being; but I do not see how I could have avoided it.

4

The Flaubert Bestiary

I attract mad people and animals.
Letter to Alfred le Poittevin, 26 May 1845

THE BEAR

Gustave was the Bear. His sister Caroline was the Rat — 'your dear rat', 'your faithful rat' she signs herself; 'little rat', 'Ah, rat, good rat, old rat', 'old rat, naughty old rat, good rat, poor old rat' he addresses her — but Gustave was the Bear. When he was only twenty, people found him 'an odd fellow, a bear, a young man out of the ordinary'; and even before his epileptic seizure and confinement at Croisset, the image had established itself: 'I am a bear and I want to stay a bear in my den, in my lair, in my skin, in my old bear's skin; I want to live quietly, far away from the bourgeois and the bourgeoises.' After his attack, the beast confirmed itself: 'I live alone, like a bear.' (The word 'alone' in this sentence is best glossed as: 'alone except for my parents, my sister, the servants, our dog, Caroline's goat, and my regular visits from Alfred le Poittevin'.)

He recovered, he was allowed to travel; in December 1850 he wrote to his mother from Constantinople, expanding the image of the Bear. It now explained not just his character, but also his literary strategy:

If you participate in life, you don't see it clearly: you suffer from it

49

too much or enjoy it too much. The artist, to my way of thinking, is a monstrosity, something outside nature. All the misfortunes Providence inflicts on him come from his stubbornness in denying that maxim ... So (and this is my conclusion) I am resigned to living as I have lived: alone, with my throng of great men as my only cronies – a bear, with my bear-rug for company.

The 'throng of cronies', needless to say, aren't house-guests but companions picked from his library shelves. As for the bear-rug, he was always concerned about it: he wrote twice from the East (Constantinople, April 1850; Benisouëf, June 1850), asking his mother to take care of it. His niece Caroline also remembered this central feature of his study. She would be taken there for her lessons at one o'clock: the shutters would be closed to keep out the heat, and the darkened room filled with the smell of joss-sticks and tobacco. 'With one bound I would throw myself on the large white bearskin, which I adored, and cover its great head with kisses.'

Once you catch your bear, says the Macedonian proverb, *it will dance for you*. Gustave didn't dance; Flaubear was nobody's bear. (How would you fiddle that into French? *Gourstave*, perhaps.)

BEAR: Generally called Martin. Quote the story of the old soldier who saw that a watch had fallen into a bear-pit, climbed down into it, and was eaten.

Dictionnaire des idées reçues

Gustave is other animals as well. In his youth he is clusters of beasts: hungry to see Ernest Chevalier, he is 'a lion, a tiger – a tiger from India, a boa constrictor' (1841); feeling a rare plenitude of strength, he is 'an ox, sphinx, bittern, elephant, whale' (1841). Subsequently, he takes them one at a time. He is an oyster in its shell (1845); a snail in its shell (1851); a hedgehog rolling up to protect itself (1853, 1857). He is a literary lizard basking in the sun of Beauty (1846), and a warbler with a shrill cry which hides in the depths of the woods and is heard only by itself (also 1846). He becomes as soft and nervous as a cow (1867); he feels as worn out as a donkey (1867); yet still he splashes in the Seine like a porpoise (1870). He works like a mule (1852); he lives a life which would kill three rhinos (1872); he works 'like XV oxen' (1878); though he advises Louise Colet to burrow away at her work like a mole (1853). To Louise he resembles 'a wild buffalo of the American prairie' (1846). To George Sand, however, he seems 'gentle as a lamb' (1866) — which he denies (1869) — and the pair of them chatter away like magpies (1866); ten years later, at her funeral, he weeps like a calf (1876). Alone in his study, he finishes the story he wrote especially for her, the story about the parrot; he bellows it out 'like a gorilla' (1876).

He flirts occasionally with the rhinoceros and the camel as self-images, but mainly, secretly, essentially, he is the Bear: a stubborn bear (1852), a bear thrust deeper into bearishness by the stupidity of his age (1853), a mangy bear (1854), even a stuffed bear (1869); and so on down to the very last year of his life, when he is still 'roaring as loudly as any bear in its cave' (1880). Note that in *Hérodias*, Flaubert's last completed work, the imprisoned prophet Iaokanann, when ordered to stop howling his denunciations against a corrupt world, replies that he too will continue crying out 'like a bear'.

> 'Language is like a cracked kettle on which we beat out tunes for bears to dance to, while all the time we long to move the stars to pity.'
>
> *Madame Bovary*

There were still bears around in Gourstave's time: brown bears in the Alps, reddish bears in Savoy. Bear hams were available from superior dealers in salted provisions. Alexandre Dumas ate bear steak at the Hôtel de la Poste, Marigny, in 1832; later, in his *Grand Dictionnaire de cuisine* (1870), he noted that 'Bear meat is now eaten by all the peoples of Europe'. From the chef to Their Majesties of Prussia Dumas obtained a recipe for bear's paws, Moscow style. Buy the paws skinned. Wash, salt, and marinade for three days. Casserole with bacon and vegetables for seven or eight hours; drain, wipe, sprinkle with pepper and turn in melted lard. Roll in breadcrumbs and grill for half an hour. Serve with a piquant sauce and two spoonfuls of redcurrant jelly.

It is not known whether Flaubear ever ate his namesake. He ate dromedary in Damascus in 1850. It seems a reasonable guess that if he had eaten bear he would have commented on such ipsophagy.

Exactly what species of bear was Flaubear? We can track his spoor through the Letters. At first he is just an unspecified *ours*, a bear (1841). He's still unspecified – though owner of a den – in 1843, in January 1845, and in May 1845 (by now he boasts a triple layer of fur). In June 1845 he wants to buy a painting of a bear for his room and entitle it 'Portrait of Gustave Flaubert' – 'to indicate my moral disposition and my social temperament'. So far we (and he too, perhaps) have been imagining a dark animal: an American brown bear, a Russian black bear, a reddish bear from Savoy. But in September 1845 Gustave firmly announces himself to be 'a white bear'.

Why? Is it because he's a bear who is also a white European? Is it perhaps an identity taken from the white bearskin rug on his study floor (which he first mentions in a letter to Louise Colet of August 1846, telling her that he likes to stretch out on it during the day. Maybe he chose his species so that he could lie on his rug, punning and camouflaged)? Or is this coloration indicative of a further shift away from humanity, a progression to the extremes of ursinity? The brown, the black, the reddish bear are not that far from man, from man's cities, man's friendship even. The coloured bears can mostly be tamed. But the white, the polar bear? It doesn't dance for man's pleasure; it doesn't eat berries; it can't be trapped by a weakness for honey.

Other bears are used. The Romans imported bears from Britain for their games. The Kamchatkans, a people of eastern Siberia, used to employ the intestines of bears as face-masks to protect them from the glare of the sun; and they used the sharpened shoulder-blade for cutting grass. But the white bear, *thalassarctos maritimus*, is the aristocrat of bears. Aloof, distant, stylishly diving for fish, roughly ambushing seals when they come up for air. The maritime bear. They travel great distances, carried along on floating pack-ice. One winter in the last century twelve great white bears got as far south as Iceland by this method; imagine them riding down on their melting thrones to make a terrifying, godlike landfall. William Scoresby, the Arctic explorer, noted that the liver of the bear is poisonous — the only part of any quadruped known to be so. Among zoo-keepers there is no known test for pregnancy in the polar bear. Strange facts that Flaubert might not have found strange.

> When the Yakuts, a Siberian people, meet a bear, they doff their caps, greet him, call him master, old man or grandfather, and promise not to attack him or even speak ill of him. But if he looks as though he may pounce on them, they shoot at him, and if they kill him, they cut him in pieces and roast him and regale themselves, repeating all the while, 'It is the Russians who are eating you, not us.'
>
> A.-F. Aulagnier, *Dictionnaire des Aliments et Boissons*

Were there other reasons why he chose to be a bear? The figurative sense of *ours* is much the same as in English: a rough, wild fellow. *Ours* is slang for a police cell. *Avoir ses ours*, to have one's bears, means 'to have the curse' (presumably because at such times a woman is supposed to behave like a bear with a sore head). Etymologists trace this colloquialism to the turn of the century (Flaubert doesn't use it; he prefers *the redcoats have landed*, and other humorous variations thereon. On one occasion, having worried over Louise Colet's irregularity, he finally notes with relief that Lord Palmerston has arrived). *Un ours mal léché*, a badly licked bear, is someone uncouth and misanthropic. More apt for Flaubert, *un ours* was nineteenth-century slang for a play which had been frequently submitted and turned down, but eventually accepted.

No doubt Flaubert knew La Fontaine's fable of the Bear and the Man Who Delighted in Gardens. There once was a bear, an ugly and deformed creature, who hid from the world and lived all alone in a wood. After a while he became melancholy and frantic — 'for indeed, Reason seldom resides long among Anchorites'. So he set off and met a gardener, who had also lived a hermetic life, and also longed for company. The bear moved into the gardener's hovel. The gardener had become a hermit because he could not abide fools; but since the bear spoke scarcely three words in the course of the day, he was able to get on with his work without disturbance. The bear used to go hunting, and bring home game for both of them. When the gardener went to sleep, the bear would sit beside him devotedly and chase away the flies that tried to settle on his face. One day, a fly landed on the tip of the man's nose, and declined to be driven away. The bear became extremely angry with the fly, and eventually seized a huge stone and succeeded in killing it. Unfortunately, in the process he beat the gardener's brains out.

Perhaps Louise Colet knew the story too.

THE CAMEL

If Gustave hadn't been the Bear, he might have been the Camel. In January 1852 he writes to Louise and explains, yet again, his incorrigibility: he is as he is, he cannot change, he does not have a say in the matter, he is subject to the gravity of things, that gravity 'which makes the polar bear inhabit the icy regions and the camel walk upon the sand'. Why the camel? Perhaps because it is a fine example of the Flaubertian grotesque: it cannot help being serious and comic at the same time. He reports from Cairo: 'One of the finest things is the camel. I never tire of watching this strange beast that lurches like a turkey and sways its neck like a swan. Its cry is something I wear myself out trying to imitate — I hope to bring it back with me — but it's hard to reproduce — a rattle with a kind of tremendous gargling as an accompaniment.'

The species also exhibited a character trait which was familiar to Gustave: 'I am, in both my physical and my mental activity, like the dromedary, which it is very hard to get going and very hard, once it is going, to stop; continuity is what I need, whether of rest or of motion.' This 1853 analogy, once it has got going, also proves hard to stop: it is still running in a letter to George Sand of 1868.

Chameau, camel, was slang for an old courtesan. I do not think this association would have put Flaubert off.

THE SHEEP

Flaubert loved fairs: the tumblers, the giantesses, the freaks, the dancing bears. In Marseilles he visited a quayside booth advertising 'sheep-women', who ran around while sailors tugged at their fleeces to see if they were real. This was not a high-class show: 'nothing could be stupider or filthier', he reported. He was far more impressed at the fair in Guérande, an old fortified town north-west of St Nazaire, which he visited during his walking tour of Brittany with Du Camp in 1847. A booth run by a sly peasant with a Picardy accent advertised 'a young phenomenon': it turned out to be a five-legged sheep with a tail in the shape of a trumpet. Flaubert was delighted, both with the freak and with its owner. He admired the beast rapturously; he took the owner out to dinner, assured him he would make a fortune, and advised him to write to King Louis Philippe on the matter. By the end of the evening, to Du Camp's clear disapproval, they were calling one another *tu*.

'The young phenomenon' fascinated Flaubert, and became part of his teasing vocabulary. As he and Du Camp tramped along, he would introduce his friend to the trees and the bushes with mock gravity: 'May I present the young phenomenon?' At Brest, Gustave fell in with the sly Picard and his freak once again, dined and got drunk with him, and further praised the magnificence of his animal. He was often thus overcome by frivolous manias; Du Camp waited for this one to run its course like a fever.

The following year, in Paris, Du Camp was ill, and confined to bed in his apartment. At four o'clock one afternoon he heard a commotion on the landing outside, and his door was flung open. Gustave strode in, followed by the five-legged sheep and the showman in the blue blouse. Some fair at the Invalides or the Champs-Elysées had disgorged them, and Flaubert was eager to share their rediscovery with his friend. Du Camp drily notes that the sheep 'did not conduct itself well'. Nor did Gustave − shouting for wine, leading the animal round the room and bellowing its virtues: 'The young phenomenon is three years old, has passed the Académie de Médecine, and has been honoured by visits from several crowned heads, etc.' After a quarter of an hour the sick Du Camp had had enough. 'I dismissed the sheep and its proprietor, and had my room swept.'

But the sheep had left its droppings in Flaubert's memory as well. A year before his death he was still reminding Du Camp about his surprise arrival with the young phenomenon, and still laughing as much as the day it had happened.

THE MONKEY, THE DONKEY, THE OSTRICH, THE SECOND DONKEY, AND MAXIME DU CAMP

A week ago I saw a monkey in the street jump on a donkey and try to wank him off − the donkey brayed and kicked, the monkey's owner shouted, the monkey itself squealed − apart from two or three children who laughed and me who found it very funny, no one paid any attention. When I described this to M. Bellin, the secretary at the consulate, he told me of having seen an ostrich trying to rape a donkey. Max had himself wanked off the other day in a deserted section among some ruins and said it was very good.

Letter to Louis Bouilhet, Cairo, January 15th, 1850

THE PARROT

Parrots are human to begin with; etymologically, that is. *Perroquet* is a diminutive of *Pierrot*; *parrot* comes from *Pierre*; Spanish *perico* derives from *Pedro*. For the Greeks, their ability to speak was an item in the philosophical debate over the differences between man and the animals. Aelian reports that 'the Brahmins honour them above all other birds. And they add that it is only reasonable to do so; for the parrot alone can give a good imitation of the human voice.' Aristotle and Pliny note that the bird is extremely lecherous when drunk. More pertinently, Buffon observes that it is prone to epilepsy. Flaubert knew of this fraternal weakness: the notes he took on parrots when researching *Un cœur simple* include a list of their maladies — gout, epilepsy, aphtha and throat ulcers.

To recapitulate. First there is Loulou, Félicité's parrot. Then there are the two contending stuffed parrots, one at the Hôtel-Dieu and one at Croisset. Then there are the three live parrots, two at Trouville and one at Venice; plus the sick parakeet at Antibes. As a possible source for Loulou we can, I think, eliminate the mother of a 'hideous' English family encountered by Gustave on the boat from Alexandria to Cairo: with a green eyeshade attached to her bonnet, she looked 'like a sick old parrot'.

Caroline, in her *Souvenirs intimes*, remarks that 'Félicité and her parrot really lived' and directs us towards the first Trouville parrot, that of Captain Barbey, as the true ancestor of Loulou. But this doesn't answer the more important question: how, and when, did a simple (if magnificent) living bird of the 1830s get turned into a complicated, transcendent parrot of the 1870s? We probably shan't ever find out; but we can suggest a point at which the transformation might have begun.

The second, uncompleted part of *Bouvard et Pécuchet* was to consist mainly of '*La Copie*', an enormous dossier of oddities, idiocies and self-condemning quotations, which the two clerks were solemnly to copy out for their own edification, and which Flaubert would reproduce with a more sardonic intent. Among the thousands of press cuttings he collected for possible inclusion in the dossier is the following story, clipped from *L'Opinion nationale* of June 20th, 1863:

'In Gérouville, near Arlon, there lived a man who owned a magnificent parrot. It was his sole love. As a young man, he had been the victim of an ill-starred passion; the experience had made him misanthropic, and now he lived alone with his parrot. He had taught the bird to pronounce the name of his lost love, and this name was repeated a hundred times a day. This was the bird's only talent, but in the eyes of its owner, the unfortunate Henri K—, it was a talent worth all the others. Every time he heard the sacred name pronounced by this strange voice, Henri thrilled with joy; it seemed to him like a voice from beyond the grave, something mysterious and superhuman.

'Solitude enflamed the imagination of Henri K—, and gradually the parrot began to take on a rare significance in his mind. For him it became a kind of holy bird: he would handle it with deep respect, and spend hours in rapt contemplation of it. Then the parrot, returning its master's gaze with an unflinching eye, would murmur the cabbalistic word, and Henri's soul would be filled with the memory of his lost happiness. This strange life lasted several years. One day, however, people noticed that Henri K— was looking gloomier than usual; and there was a strange, wild light in his eye. The parrot had died.

'Henri K— continued to live alone, now completely so. He had no link with the outside world. He became more and more wrapped up in himself. Sometimes he would not leave his room for days on end. He would eat whatever food was brought him, but took no notice of anyone. Gradually he began to believe that he himself had turned into a parrot. As if in imitation of the dead bird, he would squawk out the name he loved to hear; he would try walking like a parrot, perching on things, and extending his arms as if he had wings to beat.

'Sometimes, he would lose his temper and start breaking the furniture; and his family decided to send him to the *maison de santé* at Gheel. On the journey there, however, he escaped during the night. The next morning they found him perched in a tree. Persuading him to come down proved very difficult, until someone had the idea of placing at the foot of his tree an enormous parrot-cage. On seeing this, the unfortunate monomaniac climbed down and was recaptured. He is now in the *maison de santé* at Gheel.'

We know that Flaubert was struck by this newspaper story. After the line, 'gradually the parrot began to take on a rare significance in his mind', he made the following annotation: 'Change the animal: make it a dog instead of a parrot.' Some brief plan for a future work, no doubt. But when, finally, the story of Loulou and Félicité came to be written, it was the parrot which stayed in place, and the owner who was changed.

Before *Un cœur simple*, parrots flit briefly through Flaubert's work, and through his letters. Explaining to Louise the pull of foreign lands (December 11th, 1846), Gustave writes: 'When we are children, we all want to live in the country of parrots and candied dates.' Comforting a sad and discouraged Louise (March 27th, 1853), he reminds her that we are all caged birds, and that life weighs the heaviest on those with the largest wings: 'We are all to a greater or lesser degree eagles or canaries, parrots or vultures.' Denying to Louise that he is vain (December 9th, 1852), he distinguishes between Pride and Vanity: 'Pride is a wild beast which lives in caves and roams the desert; Vanity, on the other hand, is a parrot which hops from branch to branch and chatters away in full view.' Describing to Louise the heroic quest for style that *Madame Bovary* represents (April 19th, 1852), he explains: 'How many times have I fallen flat on my face, just when I thought I had it within my grasp. Still, I feel that I mustn't die without making sure that the style I can hear inside my head comes roaring out and drowns the cries of parrots and cicadas.'

In *Salammbô*, as I have already mentioned, the Carthaginian translators have parrots tattooed on their chests (a detail perhaps more apt than authentic?); in the same novel, some of the Barbarians have 'sunshades in their hands or parrots on their shoulders'; while the furnishings of Salammbô's terrace include a small ivory bed whose cushions are stuffed with parrot feathers — 'for this was a prophetic bird, consecrated to the gods'.

There are no parrots in *Madame Bovary* or *Bouvard et Pécuchet*; no entry for PERROQUET in the *Dictionnaire des idées reçues*; and only a couple of brief mentions in *La Tentation de saint Antoine*. In *Saint Julien l'hospitalier* few animal species avoid slaughter during Julien's first hunt — roosting grouse have their legs cut off, and low-flying cranes are snapped out of the sky by the huntsman's whip — but the parrot remains unmentioned and unharmed. In the second hunt, however, when Julien's ability to kill evaporates, when the animals become elusive, threatening observers of their stumbling pursuer, the parrot makes an appearance. Flashes of light in the forest, which Julien assumed to be stars low in the sky, prove to be the eyes of watching beasts: wild cats, squirrels, owls, parrots and monkeys.

And let's not forget the parrot that wasn't there. In *L'Education sentimentale* Frédéric wanders through an area of Paris wrecked by the 1848 uprising. He walks past barricades which have been torn down; he sees black pools that must be blood; houses have their blinds hanging like rags from a single nail. Here and there amid the chaos, delicate things have survived by chance. Frédéric peers in at a window. He sees a clock, some prints — and a parrot's perch.

It isn't so different, the way we wander through the past. Lost, disordered, fearful, we follow what signs there remain; we read the street names, but cannot be confident where we are. All around is wreckage. These people never stopped fighting. Then we see a house; a writer's house, perhaps. There is a plaque on the front wall. 'Gustave Flaubert, French writer, 1821-1880, lived here while — ' but then the letters shrink impossibly, as if on some optician's chart. We walk closer. We look in at a window. Yes, it's true; despite the carnage some delicate things have survived. A clock still ticks. Prints on the wall remind us that art was once appreciated here. A parrot's perch catches the eye. We look for the parrot. Where is the parrot? We still hear its voice; but all we can see is a bare wooden perch. The bird has flown.

DOGS

1 *The Dog Romantic.* This was a large Newfoundland, the property of Elisa Schlesinger. If we believe Du Camp, he was called Nero; if we believe Goncourt, he was called Thabor. Gustave met Mme Schlesinger at Trouville: he was fourteen and a half, she twenty-six. She was beautiful, her husband was rich; she wore an immense straw

hat, and her well-modelled shoulders could be glimpsed through her muslin dress. Nero, or Thabor, went everywhere with her. Gustave often followed at a discreet distance. Once, on the dunes, she opened her dress and suckled her baby. He was lost, helpless, tortured, fallen. Ever afterwards he would maintain that the brief summer of 1836 had cauterised his heart. (We are at liberty, of course, to disbelieve him. What did the Goncourts say? 'Though perfectly frank by nature, he is never wholly sincere in what he says he feels and suffers and loves.') And whom did he first tell of this passion? His schoolfriends? His mother? Mme Schlesinger herself? No: he told Nero (or Thabor). He would take the Newfoundland for walks across the Trouville sands, and in the soft secrecy of a dune he would drop down on his knees and wrap his arms around the dog. Then he would kiss it where he knew its mistress's lips had been not long before (the location of the kiss remains a matter of debate: some say on the muzzle, some say on the top of the head); he would whisper in the shaggy ear of Nero (or Thabor) the secrets he longed to whisper in the ear that lay between the muslin dress and the straw hat; and he would burst into tears.

The memory of Mme Schlesinger, and her presence too, pursued Flaubert for the rest of his life. What happened to the dog is not recorded.

2 *The Dog Practical*. Not sufficient study, to my mind, has been made of the pets which were kept at Croisset. They flicker into brief existence, sometimes with a name attached, sometimes not; we rarely know when or how they were acquired, and when or how they died. Let us assemble them:

In 1840 Gustave's sister Caroline had a goat called Souvit.
In 1840 the family had a black Newfoundland bitch called Néo (perhaps this name influenced Du Camp's memory of Mme Schlesinger's Newfoundland).
In 1853 Gustave dines alone at Croisset with an unnamed dog.
In 1854 Gustave dines with a dog named Dakno; probably the same animal as above.

In 1856-7 his niece Caroline has a pet rabbit.

In 1856 he exhibits on his lawn a stuffed crocodile he has brought back from the East: enabling it to bask in the sun again for the first time in 3,000 years.

In 1858 a wild rabbit takes up residence in the garden; Gustave forbids its slaughter.

In 1866 Gustave dines alone with a bowl of goldfish.

In 1867 the pet dog (no name, no breed) is killed by poison which has been laid down for rats.

In 1872 Gustave acquires Julio, a greyhound.

Note: If we are to complete the list of known domestic creatures to which Gustave played host, we must record that in October 1842 he suffered an infestation of crab-lice.

Of the pets listed above, the only one about which we have proper information is Julio. In April 1872 Mme Flaubert died; Gustave was left alone in the big house, having meals at a large table 'tête-à-tête with myself'. In September his friend Edmond Laporte offered him a greyhound. Flaubert hesitated, being frightened of rabies; but eventually accepted it. He named the dog Julio (in honour of Juliet Herbert? – if you wish) and quickly grew fond of it. By the end of the month he was writing to his niece that his sole distraction (thirty-six years after casting his arms round Mme Schlesinger's Newfoundland) was to embrace his 'pauvre chien'. 'His calm and his beauty make one jealous.'

The greyhound became his final companion at Croisset. An unlikely couple: the stout, sedentary novelist and the sleek racing dog. Julio's own private life began to feature in Flaubert's correspondence: he announced that the dog had become 'morganatically united' with 'a young person' of the neighbourhood. Owner and pet even got ill together: in the spring of 1879 Flaubert had rheumatism and a swollen foot, while Julio had an unspecified canine disease. 'He is exactly like a person,' Gustave wrote. 'He makes little gestures that are profoundly human.' Both of them recovered, and staggered on through the year. The winter of 1879-80 was exceptionally cold. Flaubert's housekeeper made Julio a coat out of an old pair of trousers. They got through the winter together. Flaubert died in the spring.

What happened to the dog is not recorded.

3 The Dog Figurative. Madame Bovary has a dog, given to her by a game-keeper whose chest infection has been cured by her husband. It is *une petite levrette d'Italie*: a small Italian greyhound bitch. Nabokov, who is exceedingly peremptory with all translators of Flaubert, renders this as whippet. Whether he is zoologically correct or not, he certainly loses the sex of the animal, which seems to me important. This dog is given a passing significance as . . . less than a symbol, not exactly a metaphor; call it a figure. Emma acquires the greyhound while she and Charles are still living at Tostes: the time of early, inchoate stirrings of dissatisfaction within her; the time of boredom and discontent, but not yet of corruption. She takes her greyhound for walks, and the animal becomes, tactfully, briefly, for half a paragraph or so, something more than just a dog. 'At first her thoughts would wander aimlessly, like her greyhound, which ran in circles, yapping after yellow butterflies, chasing field-mice and nibbling at poppies on the edge of a cornfield. Then, gradually, her ideas would come together until, sitting on a stretch of grass and stabbing at it with the end of her parasol, she would repeat to herself, "Oh God, why did I get married?" '

That is the first appearance of the dog, a delicate insertion; afterwards, Emma holds its head and kisses it (as Gustave had done to Nero/Thabor): the dog has a melancholy expression, and she talks to it as if to someone in need of consolation. She is talking, in other words (and in both senses), to herself. The dog's second appearance is also its last. Charles and Emma move from Tostes to Yonville – a journey which marks Emma's shift from dreams and fantasies to reality and corruption. Note also the traveller who shares the coach with them: the ironically named Monsieur Lheureux, the fancy-goods dealer and part-time usurer who finally ensnares Emma (financial corruption marks her fall as much as sexual corruption). On the journey, Emma's greyhound escapes. They spend a good quarter of an hour whistling for it, and then give up. M. Lheureux plies Emma with a foretaste of false comfort: he tells her consoling stories of lost dogs which have returned to their masters despite great distances; why, there was even one that made it all the way back to Paris from Constantinople. Emma's reaction to these stories is not recorded.

What happened to the dog is also not recorded.

4 The Dog Drowned and the Dog Fantastical. In January 1851 Flaubert and Du Camp were in Greece. They visited Marathón, Eleusis and Salamís. They met General Morandi, a soldier of fortune who had fought at Missolonghi, and who indignantly denied to them the calumny put about by the British aristocracy that Byron had deteriorated morally while in Greece: 'He was magnificent,' the General told them. 'He looked like Achilles.' Du Camp records how they visited Thermopylae and re-read their Plutarch on the battlefield. On January 12th they were heading towards Eleuthera – the two friends, a dragoman, and an armed policeman they employed as a guard – when the weather worsened. Rain fell heavily; the plain they were crossing became inundated; the policeman's Scotch terrier was suddenly carried away and drowned in a swollen torrent. The rain turned to snow, and darkness closed in. Clouds shut out the stars; their solitude was complete.

An hour passed, then another; snow gathered thickly in the folds of their clothes; they missed their road. The policeman fired some pistol shots in the air, but there was no answer. Saturated, and very cold, they faced the prospect of a night in the saddle amid inhospitable terrain. The policeman was grieving for his Scotch terrier, while the dragoman – a fellow with big, prominent eyes like a lobster's – had proved singularly incompetent throughout the trip; even his cooking had been a failure. They were riding cautiously, straining their eyes for a distant light, when the policeman shouted, 'Halt!' A dog was barking somewhere in the far distance. It was then that the dragoman displayed his sole talent: the ability to bark like a dog. He began to do so with a desperate vigour. When he stopped, they listened, and heard answering barks. The dragoman howled again. Slowly they advanced, stopping every so often to bark and be barked

64

back at, then reorienting themselves. After half an hour of marching towards the ever-loudening village dog, they eventually found shelter for the night.

What happened to the dragoman is not recorded.

Note: Is it fair to add that Gustave's journal offers a different version of the story? He agrees about the weather; he agrees about the date; he agrees that the dragoman couldn't cook (a constant offering of lamb and hard-boiled eggs drove him to lunch on dry bread). Strangely, though, he doesn't mention reading Plutarch on the battlefield. The policeman's dog (breed unidentified in Flaubert's version) wasn't carried away by a torrent; it just drowned in deep water. As for the barking dragoman, Gustave merely records that when they heard the village dog in the distance, he ordered the policeman to fire his pistol in the air. The dog barked its reply; the policeman fired again; and by this more ordinary means they progressed towards shelter.

What happened to the truth is not recorded.

5

Snap!

In the more bookish areas of English middle-class society, whenever a coincidence occurs there is usually someone at hand to comment, 'It's just like Anthony Powell.' Often the coincidence turns out, on the shortest examination, to be unremarkable: typically, it might consist of two acquaintances from school or university running into one another after a gap of several years. But the name of Powell is invoked to give legitimacy to the event; it's rather like getting the priest to bless your car.

I don't much care for coincidences. There's something spooky about them: you sense momentarily what it must be like to live in an ordered, God-run universe, with Himself looking over your shoulder and helpfully dropping coarse hints about a cosmic plan. I prefer to feel that things are chaotic, free-wheeling, permanently as well as temporarily crazy — to feel the certainty of human ignorance, brutality and folly. 'Whatever else happens,' Flaubert wrote when the Franco–Prussian war broke out, 'we shall remain stupid.' Mere boastful pessimism? Or a necessary razing of expectation before anything can be properly thought, or done, or written?

I don't even care for harmless, comic coincidences. I once went out to dinner and discovered that the seven other people present had all just finished reading *A Dance to the Music of Time*. I didn't relish this: not least because it meant that I didn't break my silence until the cheese course.

And as for coincidences in books — there's something cheap and sentimental about the device; it can't help always seeming aesthetically gimcrack. That troubadour who passes by just in time to rescue the girl from a hedgerow scuffle; the sudden but convenient Dickensian benefactors; the neat shipwreck on a foreign shore which reunites siblings and lovers. I once disparaged this lazy stratagem to a poet I met, a man presumably skilled in the coincidences of rhyme. 'Perhaps,' he replied with a genial loftiness, 'you have too prosaic a mind?'

'But surely,' I came back, rather pleased with myself, 'a prosaic mind is the best judge of prose?'

I'd ban coincidences, if I were a dictator of fiction. Well, perhaps not entirely. Coincidences would be permitted in the picaresque; that's where they belong. Go on, take them: let the pilot whose parachute has failed to open land in the haystack, let the virtuous pauper with the gangrenous foot discover the buried treasure — it's all right, it doesn't really matter ...

One way of legitimising coincidences, of course, is to call them ironies. That's what smart people do. Irony is, after all, the modern mode, a drinking companion for resonance and wit. Who could be against it? And yet sometimes I wonder if the wittiest, most resonant irony isn't just a well-brushed, well-educated coincidence.

I don't know what Flaubert thought about coincidence. I had hoped for some characteristic entry in his unflaggingly ironic *Dictionnaire des idées reçues*; but it jumps pointedly from *cognac* to *coitus*. Still, his love of irony is plain; it's one of the most modern things about him. In Egypt he was delighted to discover that *almeh*, the word for 'bluestocking', had gradually lost this original meaning and come to signify 'whore'.

Do ironies accrete around the ironist? Flaubert certainly thought so. The celebrations for the centenary of Voltaire's death in 1878 were stage-managed by the chocolate firm of Ménier. 'That poor old genius,' Gustave commented, 'how irony never quits him.' It badgered Gustave too. When he wrote of himself, 'I attract mad people and animals', perhaps he should have added 'and ironies'.

Take *Madame Bovary*. It was prosecuted for obscenity by Ernest Pinard, the advocate who also enjoys the shabby fame of leading the case against *Les Fleurs du mal*. Some years after *Bovary* had been cleared, Pinard was discovered to be the anonymous author of a collection of priapic verses. The novelist was much amused.

And then, take the book itself. Two of the best-remembered things in it are Emma's adulterous drive in the curtained cab (a passage found especially scandalous by right-thinkers), and the very last line of the novel — 'He has just received the Legion of Honour' — which confirms the bourgeois apotheosis of the pharmacist Homais. Now, the idea for the curtained cab appears to have come to Flaubert as a result of his own eccentric conduct in Paris when anxious to avoid running into Louise Colet. To avoid being recognised, he took to driving everywhere in a closed cab. Thus, he maintained his chastity by using a device he would later employ to facilitate his heroine's sexual indulgence.

With Homais's *Légion d'honneur*, it's the other way round: life imitates and ironises art. Barely ten years after that final line of *Madame Bovary* was written, Flaubert, arch anti-bourgeois and virile hater of governments, allowed himself to be created a *chevalier* of the *Légion d'honneur*. Consequently, the last line of his life parroted the last line of his masterpiece: at his funeral a picket of soldiers turned up to fire a volley over the coffin, and thus bid the state's traditional farewell to one of its most improbable and sardonic *chevaliers*.

And if you don't like these ironies, I have others.

1 DAWN AT THE PYRAMIDS

In December 1849 Flaubert and Du Camp climbed the Great Pyramid of Cheops. They had slept beside it the previous night, and rose at five to make sure of reaching the top by sunrise. Gustave washed his face in a canvas pail; a jackal howled; he smoked a pipe.

Then, with two Arabs pushing him and two pulling, he was bundled slowly up the high stones of the Pyramid to the summit. Du Camp — the first man to photograph the Sphinx — was there already. Ahead of them lay the Nile, bathed in mist, like a white sea; behind them lay the dark desert, like a petrified purple ocean. At last, a streak of orange light appeared to the east; and gradually the white sea in front of them became an immense expanse of fertile green, while the purple ocean behind turned shimmering white. The rising sun lit up the topmost stones of the Pyramid, and Flaubert, looking down at his feet, noticed a small business-card pinned in place. 'Humbert, Frotteur', it read, and gave a Rouen address.

What a moment of perfectly targeted irony. A modernist moment, too: this is the sort of exchange, in which the everyday tampers with the sublime, that we like to think of proprietorially as typical of our own wry and unfoolable age. We thank Flaubert for picking it up; in a sense, the irony wasn't there until he observed it. Other visitors might have seen the business-card as merely a piece of litter — it could have stayed there, its drawing-pins slowly rusting, for years; but Flaubert gave it function.

And if we are feeling interpretative, we can look further into this brief event. Isn't it, perhaps, a notable historical coincidence that the greatest European novelist of the nineteenth century should be introduced at the Pyramids to one of the twentieth century's most notorious fictional characters? That Flaubert, still damp from skewering boys in Cairo bath-houses, should fall on the name of Nabokov's seducer of underage American girlhood? And further, what is the profession of this single-barrelled version of Humbert Humbert? He is a *frotteur*. Literally, a French polisher; but also, the sort of sexual deviant who loves the rub of the crowd.

And that's not all. Now for the irony about the irony. It turns out, from Flaubert's travel notes, that the business-card wasn't pinned in place by Monsieur Frotteur himself; it was put there by the lithe and thoughtful Maxime du Camp, who had scampered ahead in the purple night and laid out this little mousetrap for his friend's sensibility. The balance of our response shifts with this knowledge: Flaubert becomes plodding and predictable; Du Camp becomes the wit, the dandy, the teaser of modernism before modernism has declared itself.

But then we read on again. If we turn to Flaubert's letters, we discover him, some days after the incident, writing to his mother about the *sublime surprise* of the discovery. 'And to think that I had specially brought that card all the way from Croisset and didn't even get to put it in place! The villain took advantage of my forgetfulness and discovered the wonderfully apposite business-card in the bottom of my folding hat.' So, ever stranger: Flaubert, when he left home, was already preparing the special effects which would later appear entirely characteristic of how he perceived the world. Ironies breed; realities recede. And why, just out of interest, did he take his folding hat to the Pyramids?

2 DESERT ISLAND DISCS

Gustave used to look back on his summer holidays at Trouville — spent between Captain Barbey's parrot and Mme Schlesinger's dog — as among the few tranquil times of his life. Reminiscing from the autumn of his mid-twenties, he told Louise Colet that 'the greatest events of my life have been a few thoughts, reading, certain sunsets by the sea at Trouville, and conversations of five or six hours on the trot with a friend [Alfred le Poittevin] who is now married and lost to me.'

In Trouville he met Gertrude and Harriet Collier, daughters of a British naval attaché. Both, it seems, became enamoured of him. Harriet gave him her portrait, which hung over the chimney-piece at Croisset; but it was of Gertrude that he was fonder. Her feelings for him may be guessed at from a text she wrote decades later, after Gustave's death. Adopting the style of romantic fiction, and using disguised names, she boasts that 'I loved him passionately, adoringly. Years have passed over my head but I have never felt the worship, the love and yet the fear that took possession of my soul then. Something told me I should never be his . . . But I knew, in the deepest recesses of my heart, how truly I could love him, honour him and obey him.'

Gertrude's lush memoir might well be fanciful: what, after all, is more sentimentally alluring than a dead genius and an adolescent beach holiday? But perhaps it wasn't. Gustave and Gertrude kept in distant touch along the decades. He sent her a copy of *Madame Bovary* (she thanked him, pronounced the novel 'hideous', and quoted at him Philip James Bailey, author of *Festus*, on the writer's duty to give moral instruction to the reader); and forty years after that first meeting in Trouville she came to visit him at Croisset. The handsome, blond cavalier of her youth was now bald and red-faced, with only a couple of teeth left in his head. But his gallantry remained in good health. 'My old friend, my youth,' he wrote to her afterwards, 'during the long years I have lived without knowing your whereabouts, there was perhaps not a single day when I did not think of you.'

During the course of those long years (in 1847, to be precise, the year after Flaubert was recalling his Trouville sunsets to Louise) Gertrude had promised to love, honour and obey someone else: an English economist called Charles Tennant. While Flaubert slowly attained European fame as a novelist, Gertrude was herself to publish a book: an edition of her grandfather's journal, called *France on the Eve of the Great Revolution*. She died in 1918 at the age of ninety-nine; and she had a daughter, Dorothy, who married the explorer Henry Morton Stanley.

On one of Stanley's trips to Africa, his party got into difficulties. The explorer was obliged gradually to discard all his unnecessary belongings. It was, in a way, a reverse, real-life version of 'Desert Island Discs': instead of being equipped with things to make life in the tropics more bearable, Stanley was having to get rid of things to survive there. Books were obviously supernumerary, and he began jettisoning them until he got down to those two which every guest on 'Desert Island Discs' is furnished with as a bare, civilised minimum: the Bible and Shakespeare. Stanley's third book, the one he threw out before reducing himself to this final minimum, was *Salammbô*.

3 THE SNAP OF COFFINS

The weary, valetudinarian tone of Flaubert's letter to Louise Colet about the sunsets was not a pose. 1846, after all, was the year when first his father and then his sister Caroline had died. 'What a house!' he wrote. 'What a hell!' All night Gustave watched beside his sister's corpse: she lying in her white wedding-dress, he sitting and reading Montaigne.

On the morning of the funeral, he gave her a last farewell kiss as she lay in her coffin. For the second time in three months he heard the battering sound of hobnailed boots climbing the wooden stairs to fetch a body. Mourning was scarcely possible that day: practicalities supervened. There was a lock of Caroline's hair to be cut, and plaster casts of her face and hands to be taken: 'I saw the great paws of those louts touching her and covering her face with plaster.' Great louts are necessary for funerals.

The trail to the cemetery was familiar from the time before. At the graveside Caroline's husband broke down. Gustave watched as the coffin was lowered. Suddenly, it got stuck: the hole had been dug too narrow. The gravediggers got hold of the coffin and shook it; they pulled it this way and that, twisted it, hacked at it with a spade, levered at it with crowbars; but still it wouldn't move. Finally, one of them placed his foot flat on the box, right over Caroline's face, and forced it down into the grave.

Gustave had a bust made of that face; it presided over his study all his working life, until his own death, in the same house, in 1880. Maupassant helped lay out the body. Flaubert's niece asked for the traditional cast of the writer's hand to be taken. This proved impossible: the fist was too tightly clenched in its terminal seizure.

The procession set off, first to the church at Canteleu, then to the Cimetière Monumental, where the picket of soldiers fired its ludicrous gloss on the last line of *Madame Bovary*. A few words were spoken, then the coffin was lowered. It got stuck. The width had been correctly judged on this occasion; but the gravediggers had skimped on the length. Sons of louts grappled with the coffin in vain; they could neither cram it in nor twist it out. After a few embarrassed minutes the mourners slowly departed, leaving Flaubert jammed into the ground at an oblique angle.

The Normans are a famously stingy race, and doubtless their gravediggers are no exception; perhaps they resent every superfluous sod they cut, and maintained this resentment as a professional tradition from 1846 to 1880. Perhaps Nabokov had read Flaubert's letters before writing *Lolita*. Perhaps H. M. Stanley's admiration for Flaubert's African novel isn't entirely surprising. Perhaps what we read as brute coincidence, silky irony, or brave, far-sighted modernism, looked quite different at the time. Flaubert took Monsieur Humbert's business-card all the way from Rouen to the Pyramids. Was it meant to be a chuckling advertisement for his own sensibility; a tease about the gritty, unpolishable surface of the desert; or might it just have been a joke on us?

6

Emma Bovary's Eyes

Let me tell you why I hate critics. Not for the normal reasons: that they're failed creators (they usually aren't; they may be failed critics, but that's another matter); or that they're by nature carping, jealous and vain (they usually aren't; if anything, they might better be accused of over-generosity, of upgrading the second-rate so that their own fine discriminations thereby appear the rarer). No, the reason I hate critics — well, some of the time — is that they write sentences like this:

> Flaubert does not build up his characters, as did Balzac, by objective, external description; in fact, so careless is he of their outward appearance that on one occasion he gives Emma brown eyes (14); on another deep black eyes (15); and on another blue eyes (16).

This precise and disheartening indictment was drawn up by the late Dr Enid Starkie, Reader Emeritus in French Literature at the University of Oxford, and Flaubert's most exhaustive British biographer. The numbers in her text refer to footnotes in which she spears the novelist with chapter and verse.

I once heard Dr Starkie lecture, and I'm glad to report that she had an atrocious French accent; one of those deliveries full of dame-school confidence and absolutely no ear, swerving between workaday correctness and farcical error, often within the same word. Naturally, this didn't affect her competence to teach at the University of Oxford, because until quite recently the place preferred to treat modern languages as if they were dead: this made them more respectable, more like the distant perfections of Latin and Greek. Even so, it did strike me as peculiar that someone who lived by French literature should be so calamitously inadequate at making the basic words of the language sound as they did when her subjects, her heroes (her paymasters, too, you could say) first pronounced them.

You might think this a cheap revenge on a dead lady critic simply for pointing out that Flaubert didn't have a very reliable notion of Emma Bovary's eyes. But then I don't hold with the precept *de mortuis nil nisi bonum* (I speak as a doctor, after all); and it's hard to underestimate the irritation when a critic points out something like that to you. The irritation isn't with Dr Starkie, not at first — she was only, as they say, doing her job — but with Flaubert. So that painstaking genius couldn't even keep the eyes of his most famous character a consistent colour? *Ha*. And then, unable to be cross with him for long, you shift your feelings over to the critic.

I must confess that in all the times *I* read *Madame Bovary*, I never noticed the heroine's rainbow eyes. Should I have? Would you? Was I perhaps too busy noticing things that Dr Starkie was missing (though what they might have been I can't for the moment think)? Put it another way: is there a perfect reader somewhere, a total reader? Does Dr Starkie's reading of *Madame Bovary* contain all the responses which I have when I read the book, and then add a whole lot more, so that my reading is in a way pointless? Well, I hope not. My reading might be pointless in terms of the history of literary criticism; but it's not pointless in terms of pleasure. I can't prove that lay readers enjoy books more than professional critics; but I can tell you one advantage we have over them. We can forget. Dr Starkie and her kind are cursed with memory: the books they teach and write about can never fade from their brains. They become family. Perhaps this is why some critics develop a faintly patronising tone towards their subjects. They act as if Flaubert, or Milton, or Wordsworth were some tedious old aunt in a rocking chair, who smelt of stale powder, was only interested in the past, and hadn't said anything new for years. Of course, it's her house, and everybody's living in it rent free; but even so, surely it is, well, you know . . . *time*?

Whereas the common but passionate reader is allowed to forget; he can go away, be unfaithful with other writers, come back and be entranced again. Domesticity need never intrude on the relationship; it may be sporadic, but when there it is always intense. There's none of the daily rancour which develops when people live bovinely together. I never find myself, fatigue in the voice, reminding Flaubert to hang up the bathmat or use the lavatory brush. Which is what Dr Starkie can't help herself doing. Look, writers aren't *perfect*, I want to cry; any more than husbands and wives are perfect. The only unfailing rule is, if they seem so, they can't be. I never thought my wife was perfect. I loved her, but I never deceived myself. I remember . . . But I'll keep that for another time.

I'll remember instead another lecture I once attended, some years ago at the Cheltenham Literary Festival. It was given by a professor from Cambridge, Christopher Ricks, and it was a very shiny performance. His bald head was shiny; his black shoes were shiny; and his lecture was very shiny indeed. Its theme was Mistakes in Literature and Whether They Matter. Yevtushenko, for example, apparently made a howler in one of his poems about the American nightingale. Pushkin was quite wrong about the sort of military dress worn at balls. John Wain was wrong about the Hiroshima pilot. Nabokov was wrong — rather surprising, this — about the phonetics of the name Lolita. There were other examples: Coleridge, Yeats and Browning were some of those caught out not knowing a hawk from a handsaw, or not even knowing what a handsaw was in the first place.

Two examples particularly struck me. The first was a remarkable discovery about *Lord of the Flies*. In the famous scene where Piggy's spectacles are used for the rediscovery of fire, William Golding got his optics wrong. Completely back to front, in fact. Piggy is short-sighted; and the spectacles he would have been prescribed for this condition could not possibly have been used as burning glasses. Whichever way you held them, they would have been quite unable to make the rays of the sun converge.

The second example concerned 'The Charge of the Light Brigade'. 'Into the valley of Death/Rode the six hundred.' Tennyson wrote the poem very quickly, after reading a report in *The Times* which included the phrase 'someone had blundered'. He also relied on an earlier account which had mentioned '607 sabres'. Subsequently, however, the number of those who took part in what Camille Rousset called *ce terrible et sanglant steeplechase* was officially corrected to 673. 'Into the valley of Death/Rode the six hundred and seventy-three'? Not quite enough swing to it, somehow. Perhaps it could have been rounded up to seven hundred – still not quite accurate, but at least more accurate? Tennyson considered the matter and decided to leave the poem as he had written it: 'Six is much better than seven hundred (as I think) metrically so keep it.'

Not putting '673' or '700' or '*c.*700' instead of '600' hardly seems to qualify as a Mistake to me. The shakiness of Golding's optics, on the other hand, must definitely be classed as an error. The next question is, Does it matter? As far as I can remember Professor Ricks's lecture, his argument was that if the factual side of literature becomes unreliable, then ploys such as irony and fantasy become much harder to use. If you don't know what's true, or what's meant to be true, then the value of what isn't true, or isn't meant to be true, becomes diminished. This seems to me a very sound argument; though I do wonder to how many cases of literary mistake it actually applies. With Piggy's glasses, I should think that a) very few people apart from oculists, opticians and bespectacled professors of English would notice; and b) when they do notice, they merely detonate the error – like blowing up a small bomb with a controlled explosion. What's more, this detonation (which takes place on a remote beach, with only a dog as witness) doesn't set fire to other parts of the novel.

Mistakes like Golding's are 'external mistakes' – disparities between what the book claims to be the case, and what we know the reality to be; often they merely indicate a lack of specific technical

77

knowledge on the writer's part. The sin is pardonable. What, though, about 'internal mistakes', when the writer claims two incompatible things within his own creation? Emma's eyes are brown, Emma's eyes are blue. Alas, this can be put down only to incompetence, to sloppy literary habits. I read the other day a well-praised first novel in which the narrator — who is both sexually inexperienced and an amateur of French literature — comically rehearses to himself the best way to kiss a girl without being rebuffed: 'With a slow, sensual, irresistible strength, draw her gradually towards you while gazing into her eyes as if you had just been given a copy of the first, suppressed edition of *Madame Bovary*.'

I thought this was quite neatly put, indeed rather amusing. The only trouble is, there's no such thing as a 'first, suppressed edition of *Madame Bovary*'. The novel, as I should have thought was tolerably well known, first appeared serially in the *Revue de Paris*; then came the prosecution for obscenity; and only after the acquittal was the work published in book form. I expect the young novelist (it seems unfair to give his name) was thinking of the 'first, suppressed edition' of *Les Fleurs du mal*. No doubt he'll get it right in time for his second edition; if there is one.

Eyes of brown, eyes of blue. Does it matter? Not, does it matter if the writer contradicts himself; but, does it matter what colour they are anyway? I feel sorry for novelists when they have to mention women's eyes: there's so little choice, and whatever colouring is decided upon inevitably carries banal implications. Her eyes are blue: innocence and honesty. Her eyes are black: passion and depth. Her eyes are green: wildness and jealousy. Her eyes are brown: reliability and common sense. Her eyes are violet: the novel is by Raymond Chandler. How can you escape all this without some haversack of a parenthesis about the lady's character? Her eyes are mud-coloured; her eyes changed hue according to the contact lenses she wore; he never looked her in the eye. Well, take your pick. My wife's eyes were greeny-blue, which makes her story a long one. And so I suspect that in the writer's moments of private candour, he probably admits the pointlessness of describing eyes. He slowly imagines the character, moulds her into shape, and then — probably the last thing of all — pops a pair of glass eyes into those empty sockets. Eyes? Oh yes, she'd better have eyes, he reflects, with a weary courtesy.

Bouvard and Pécuchet, during their investigations into literature, find that they lose respect for an author when he strays into error. I am more surprised by how few mistakes writers make. So the Bishop of Liège dies fifteen years before he should: does this invalidate *Quentin Durward*? It's a trivial offence, something tossed to the reviewers. I see the novelist at the stern rail of a cross-Channel ferry, throwing bits of gristle from his sandwich to the hovering gulls.

I was too far away to observe what colour Enid Starkie's eyes were; all I remember of her is that she dressed like a matelot, walked like a scrum-half, and had an atrocious French accent. But I'll tell you another thing. The Reader Emeritus in French Literature at the University of Oxford and Honorary Fellow of Somerville College, who was 'well known for her studies of the lives and works of writers such as Baudelaire, Rimbaud, Gautier, Eliot and Gide' (I quote her dust-wrapper; first edition, of course), who devoted two large books and many years of her life to the author of *Madame Bovary*, chose as frontispiece to her first volume a portrait of 'Gustave Flaubert by an unknown painter'. It's the first thing we see; it is, if you like, the moment at which Dr Starkie introduces us to Flaubert. The only trouble is, it isn't him. It's a portrait of Louis Bouilhet, as everyone from the *gardienne* of Croisset onwards and upwards will tell you. So what do we make of that once we've stopped chuckling?

Perhaps you still think I'm merely being vengeful towards a dead scholar who can't answer for herself. Well, maybe I am. But then, *quis custodiet ipsos custodes*? And I'll tell you something else. I've just reread *Madame Bovary*.

On one occasion he gives Emma brown eyes (14); on another deep black eyes (15); and on another blue eyes (16).

And the moral of it all, I suppose, is: Never take fright at a footnote.

Here are the six references Flaubert makes to Emma Bovary's eyes in the course of the book. It is clearly a subject of some importance to the novelist:

1 (Emma's first appearance) 'In so far as she was beautiful, this beauty lay in her eyes: although they were brown, they would appear black because of her lashes ... '

2 (Described by her adoring husband early in their marriage) 'Her eyes seemed bigger to him, especially when she was just waking up and fluttered her lids several times in succession; they were black when she was in shadow and dark blue in full daylight; and they seemed to contain layer upon layer of colours, which were thicker in hue deep down, and became lighter towards the enamel-like surface.'

3 (At a candlelit ball) 'Her black eyes appeared even blacker.'

4 (On first meeting Leon) 'Fixing him with her large, wide-open black eyes'.

5 (Indoors, as she appears to Rodolphe when he first examines her) 'Her black eyes'.

6 (Emma looking in a mirror, indoors, in the evening; she has just been seduced by Rodolphe) 'Her eyes had never been so large, so black, nor contained such depth.'

How did the critic put it? 'Flaubert does not build up characters, as did Balzac, by objective, external description; in fact, so careless is he of their outward appearance that ... ' It would be interesting to compare the time spent by Flaubert making sure that his heroine had the rare and difficult eyes of a tragic adulteress with the time spent by Dr Starkie in carelessly selling him short.

And one final thing, just to make absolutely sure. Our earliest substantial source of knowledge about Flaubert is Maxime du Camp's *Souvenirs littéraires* (Hachette, Paris, 1882–3, 2 vols): gossipy, vain, self-justifying and unreliable, yet historically essential. On page 306 of the first volume (Remington & Co., London, 1893, no translator credited) Du Camp describes in great detail the woman on whom Emma Bovary was based. She was, he tells us, the second wife of a medical officer from Bon-Lecours, near Rouen:

This second wife was not beautiful; she was small, had dull yellow hair, and a face covered with freckles. She was full of pretension, and despised her husband, whom she considered a fool. Round and fair in person, her small bones were well-covered, and in her carriage and her general bearing there were flexible, undulating movements, like those of an eel. Her voice, vulgarised by its Lower Normandy accent, was full of caressing tones, and her eyes, of uncertain colour, green, grey, or blue, according to the light, had a pleading expression, which never left them.

Dr Starkie appears to have been serenely unaware of this enlightening passage. All in all, it seems a magisterial negligence towards a writer who must, one way and another, have paid a lot of her gas bills. Quite simply, it makes me furious. Now do you understand why I hate critics? I could try and describe to you the expression in my eyes at this moment; but they are far too discoloured with rage.

7

Cross Channel

Listen. *Rattarattarattaratta*. And then — shhh — over there. *Fattafatta-fattafatta*. And again. *Rattarattarattaratta* — *fattafattafattafatta*. A soft November swell has set the tables rattling metallically at one another across the bar. An insistent approach from a table close at hand; a pause while some unheard throb shifts across the boat; and then a softer reply from the other side. Call and response, call and response; like a pair of mechanical birds in a cage. Listen to the pattern: *rattarattarattaratta fattafattafattafatta rattarattarattaratta fattafattafatta-fatta*. Continuity, stability, mutual reliance, it says; yet a change of wind or tide could end it all.

The curving windows at the stern are freckled with spray; through one of them you can make out a set of fat capstans and a listless macaroni of sodden rope. The seagulls have long since given up on this ferry. They cawed us out of Newhaven, had a look at the weather, noted the lack of sandwich packs on the rear promenade, and turned back. Who can blame them? They could have followed us the four hours to Dieppe in the hope of picking up trade on the way back; but that makes for a ten-hour day. By now they will be digging worms on some damp football pitch in Rottingdean.

Beneath the window is a bilingual rubbish bin with a spelling mistake. The top line says PAPIERS (how official the French sounds: 'Driving licence! Identity card!' it seems to command). The English translation underneath reads LITTERS. What a difference a single consonant makes. The first time Flaubert saw his name advertised — as the author of *Madame Bovary*, shortly to be serialised in the *Revue de Paris* — it was spelt Faubert. 'If I make an appearance one day, it will be in full armour,' had been his boast; but even in full armour the armpit and the groin are never completely protected. As he pointed out to Bouilhet, the *Revue*'s version of his name was only a letter away from an unwanted commercial pun: Faubet being the name of a grocer in the rue Richelieu, just opposite the Comédie-Française. 'Even before I've appeared, they skin me alive.'

I like these out-of-season crossings. When you're young you prefer the vulgar months, the fullness of the seasons. As you grow older you learn to like the in-between times, the months that can't make up their minds. Perhaps it's a way of admitting that things can't ever bear the same certainty again. Or perhaps it's just a way of admitting a preference for empty ferries.

There can't be more than half a dozen people in the bar. One of them is stretched out on a banquette; the lulling rattle of the tables is coaxing its first snore from him. At this time of the year there are no school parties; the video games, disco and cinema are silent; even the barman chats.

This is the third time I've made the trip in a year. November, March, November. Just for a couple of nights in Dieppe: though I sometimes take the car and get down to Rouen. It's not long, but it's enough to make the change. It *is* a change. The light over the Channel, for instance, looks quite different from the French side: clearer, yet more volatile. The sky is a theatre of possibilities. I'm not romanticising. Go into the art galleries along the Normandy coast and you'll see what the local painters liked to paint, over and over again: the view north. A strip of beach, the sea, and the eventful sky. English painters never did the same, clustering at Hastings or Margate or Eastbourne to gaze out at a grumpy, monotonous Channel.

I don't just go for the light. I go for those things you forget about until you see them again. The way they butcher meat. The seriousness of their *pharmacies*. The behaviour of their children in restaurants. The road signs (France is the only country I know where drivers are warned about beetroot on the road: BETTERAVES, I once saw in a red warning triangle, with a picture of a car slipping out of control). *Beaux-arts* town halls. Wine-tasting in smelly chalk-caves by the side of the road. I could go on, but that's enough, or I'll soon be babbling about lime trees and *pétanque* and eating bread dipped in rough red wine — what they call *la soupe à perroquet*, parrot soup. Everyone has a private list, and those of other people quickly appear vain and sentimental. I read a list the other day headed 'What I Like'. It went: 'Salad, cinnamon, cheese, pimento, marzipan, the smell of new-cut hay [would you read on?] ... roses, peonies, lavender, champagne, loosely-held political convictions, Glenn Gould ... ' The list, which is by Roland Barthes, continues, as lists do. One item you approve, the next stirs irritation. After 'Médoc wine' and 'having change', Barthes approves of '*Bouvard et Pécuchet*'. Good; fine; we'll read on. What's next? 'Walking in sandals on the lanes of south-west France.' It's enough to make you drive all the way to south-west France and strew some beetroot on the lanes.

My list mentions *pharmacies*. They always seem more single-minded in France. They don't stock beachballs or colour film or snorkelling equipment or burglar alarms. The assistants know what they are doing, and never try to sell you barley sugar on the way out. I find myself deferring to them as if they were consultants.

My wife and I once went into a *pharmacie* in Montauban and requested a packet of bandages. What was it for, they asked. Ellen tapped her heel, where the strap of a new pair of sandals had rubbed up a blister. The *pharmacien* came out from behind his counter, sat her down, removed her sandal with the tenderness of a foot-fetishist, examined her heel, cleaned it with a piece of gauze, stood up, turned to me gravely, as if there were something which really ought to be kept from my wife, and quietly explained, '*That*, Monsieur, is a blister.' The spirit of Homais still reigns, I thought, as he sold us a packet of bandages.

The spirit of Homais: progress, rationalism, science, fraud. 'We must march with the century' are almost his first words; and he marches all the way to the *Légion d'honneur*. When Emma Bovary dies, her body is watched over by two people: the priest, and Homais the *pharmacien*. Representing the old orthodoxy and the new. It's like some piece of nineteenth-century allegorical sculpture: Religion and Science Watching Together over the Body of Sin. From a painting by G.F. Watts. Except that both the cleric and the man of science manage to fall asleep over the body. United at first only by philosophic error, they quickly establish the deeper unity of joint snorers.

Flaubert didn't believe in progress: especially not in moral progress, which is all that matters. The age he lived in was stupid; the new age, brought in by the Franco-Prussian war, would be even stupider. Of course some things would change: the spirit of Homais was winning. Soon everybody with a club foot would be entitled to a misconceived operation which would lead to an amputated leg; but what did that signify? 'The whole dream of democracy', he wrote, 'is to raise the proletariat to the level of stupidity attained by the bourgeoisie.'

That line often makes people edgy. Isn't it perfectly fair? Over the last hundred years the proletariat has schooled itself in the pretensions of the bourgeoisie; while the bourgeoisie, less confident of its ascendancy, has become more sly and deceitful. Is this progress? Study a packed cross-Channel ferry if you want to see a modern ship of fools. There they all are: working out the profit on their duty-free; having more drinks at the bar than they want; playing the fruit machines; aimlessly circling the deck; making up their minds how honest to be at customs; waiting for the next order from the ship's crew as if the crossing of the Red Sea depended on it. I do not criticise, I merely observe; and I'm not sure what I would think if everyone lined the rail to admire the play of light on the water and started discussing Boudin. I am no different, by the way: I stock up on duty-free and await orders like the rest of them. My point is merely this: Flaubert was right.

The fat lorry-driver on the banquette is snoring like a pasha. I've fetched myself another whisky; I hope you don't mind. Just getting braced to tell you about ... what? about whom? Three stories contend within me. One about Flaubert, one about Ellen, one about myself. My own is the simplest of the three — it hardly amounts to more than a convincing proof of my existence — and yet I find it the hardest to begin. My wife's is more complicated, and more urgent; yet I resist that too. Keeping the best for last, as I was saying earlier? I don't think so; rather the opposite, if anything. But by the time I tell you her story I want you to be prepared: that's to say, I want you to have had enough of books, and parrots, and lost letters, and bears, and the opinions of Dr Enid Starkie, and even the opinions of Dr Geoffrey Braithwaite. Books are not life, however much we might prefer it if they were. Ellen's is a true story; perhaps it is even the reason why I am telling you Flaubert's story instead.

You expect something from me too, don't you? It's like that nowadays. People assume they own part of you, on no matter how small an acquaintance; while if you are reckless enough to write a book, this puts your bank account, your medical records, and the state of your marriage irrevocably into the public domain. Flaubert disapproved. 'The artist must manage to make posterity believe that he never existed.' For the religious, death destroys the body and liberates the spirit; for the artist, death destroys the personality and liberates the work. That's the theory, anyway. Of course, it frequently goes wrong. Look what happened to Flaubert: a century after his death Sartre, like some brawny, desperate lifeguard, spent ten years beating on his chest and blowing into his mouth; ten years trying to yank him back to consciousness, just so that he could sit him up on the sands and tell him exactly what he thought of him.

And what do people think of him now? How do they think of him? As a bald man with a drooping moustache; as the hermit of Croisset, the man who said '*Madame Bovary, c'est moi*'; as the incorrigible aesthete, the bourgeois bourgeoisophobe? Confident scraps of wisdom, hand-me-down summaries for those in a hurry. Flaubert would hardly have been surprised at the lazy rush to understand. It was an impulse out of which he made a whole book (or at least a whole appendix): the *Dictionnaire des idées reçues*.

At the simplest level, his Dictionary is a catalogue of clichés (DOG: *Especially created to save its master's life. A dog is man's best friend*) and cod definitions (CRAYFISH: *Female of the lobster*). Beyond this it's a handbook of fake advice, both social (LIGHT: *Always say* Fiat lux! *when lighting a candle*) and aesthetic (RAILWAY STATIONS: *Always go into ecstasies about them; cite them as models of architecture*). Sometimes the manner is sly and teasing, at others so challengingly straight-faced that you find yourself half-believing it (MACARONI: *When prepared in the Italian style, is served with the fingers*). It reads like a confirmation present specially written by a malicious, rakehell uncle for a serious-minded adolescent with ambitions to get on in society. Study it carefully and you would never say anything wrong, while never getting anything right (HALBERD: *When you see a heavy cloud, never fail to say: 'It's going to rain halberds.' In Switzerland, all the men carry halberds.* ABSINTHE: *Extremely violent poison: a single glass and you're dead. Always drunk by journalists while writing their articles. Has killed more soldiers than the Bedouin*).

Flaubert's Dictionary offers a course in irony: from entry to entry, you can see him applying it in various thicknesses, like a cross-Channel painter darkening the sky with another wash. It tempts me to write a Dictionary of Accepted Ideas about Gustave himself. Just a short one: a booby-trapped pocket guide; something straight-faced yet misleading. The received wisdom in pellet form, with some of the pellets poisoned. This is the attraction, and also the danger, of irony: the way it permits a writer to be seemingly absent from his work, yet in fact hintingly present. You *can* have your cake and eat it; the only trouble is, you get fat.

What might we say of Flaubert in this new Dictionary? We might set him down, perhaps, as a 'bourgeois individualist'; yes, that sounds smug enough, dishonest enough. It's a characterisation which always remains unshaken by the fact that Flaubert loathed the bourgeoisie. And how about 'individualist', or its equivalent? 'In the ideal I have of Art, I think that one must not show one's own, and that the artist must no more appear in his work than God does in nature. Man is nothing, the work of art everything ... It would be very pleasant for me to say what I think and relieve Monsieur Gustave Flaubert's feelings by means of such utterances; but what is the importance of the said gentleman?'

This demand for authorial absence ran deeper still. Some writers ostensibly agree with the principle, yet sneak in at the back door and cosh the reader with a highly personal style. The murder is perfectly executed, except that the baseball bat left at the scene of the crime is sticky with fingerprints. Flaubert is different. He believed in style; more than anyone. He worked doggedly for beauty, sonority, exactness; perfection – but never the monogrammed perfection of a writer like Wilde. Style is a function of theme. Style is not imposed on subject-matter, but arises from it. Style is truth to thought. The correct word, the true phrase, the perfect sentence are always 'out there' somewhere; the writer's task is to locate them by whatever means he can. For some this means no more than a trip to the supermarket and a loading-up of the metal basket; for others it means being lost on a plain in Greece, in the dark, in snow, in the rain, and finding what you seek only by some rare trick such as barking like a dog.

In our pragmatic and knowing century we probably find such ambition a little provincial (well, Turgenev did call Flaubert naïve). We no longer believe that language and reality 'match up' so congruently – indeed, we probably think that words give birth to things as much as things give birth to words. But if we find Flaubert naïve or – more likely – unsuccessful, we shouldn't patronise his seriousness or his bold loneliness. This was, after all, the century of Balzac and of Hugo, with orchidaceous Romanticism at one end of it and gnomic symbolism at the other. Flaubert's planned invisibility in a century of babbling personalities and shrieking styles might be characterised in one of two ways: as classical, or modern. Looking back to the seventeenth century, or forward to the late twentieth century. Contemporary critics who pompously reclassify all novels and plays and poems as texts – the author to the guillotine! – shouldn't skip lightly over Flaubert. A century before them he was preparing texts and denying the significance of his own personality.

'The author in his book must be like God in his universe, everywhere present and nowhere visible.' Of course, this has been keenly misread in our century. Look at Sartre and Camus. God is dead, they told us, and therefore so is the God-like novelist. Omniscience is impossible, man's knowledge is partial, therefore the novel

88

itself must be partial. That sounds not just splendid, but logical as well. But is it either? The novel, after all, didn't arise when belief in God arose; nor, for that matter, is there much correlation between those novelists who believed most strongly in the omniscient narrator and those who believed most strongly in the omniscient creator. I cite George Eliot alongside Flaubert.

More to the point, the assumed divinity of the nineteenth-century novelist was only ever a technical device; and the partiality of the modern novelist is just as much a ploy. When a contemporary narrator hesitates, claims uncertainty, misunderstands, plays games and falls into error, does the reader in fact conclude that reality is being more authentically rendered? When the writer provides two different endings to his novel (why two? why not a hundred?), does the reader seriously imagine he is being 'offered a choice' and that the work is reflecting life's variable outcomes? Such a 'choice' is never real, because the reader is obliged to consume both endings. In life, we make a decision — or a decision makes us — and we go one way; had we made a different decision (as I once told my wife; though I don't think she was in a condition to appreciate my wisdom), we would have been elsewhere. The novel with two endings doesn't reproduce this reality: it merely takes us down two diverging paths. It's a form of cubism, I suppose. And that's all right; but let's not deceive ourselves about the artifice involved.

After all, if novelists truly wanted to simulate the delta of life's possibilities, this is what they'd do. At the back of the book would be a set of sealed envelopes in various colours. Each would be clearly marked on the outside: Traditional Happy Ending; Traditional Unhappy Ending; Traditional Half-and-Half Ending; Deus ex Machina; Modernist Arbitrary Ending; End of the World Ending; Cliffhanger Ending; Dream Ending; Opaque Ending; Surrealist Ending; and so on. You would be allowed only one, and would have to destroy the envelopes you didn't select. *That*'s what I call offering the reader a choice of endings; but you may find me quite unreasonably literal-minded.

As for the hesitating narrator — look, I'm afraid you've run into one right now. It might be because I'm English. You'd guessed that, at least — that I'm English? I . . . I . . . Look at that seagull up there. I hadn't spotted him before. Slipstreaming away, waiting for the bits of gristle from the sandwiches. Listen, I hope you won't think this rude, but I really must take a turn on deck; it's becoming quite stuffy in the bar here. Why don't we meet on the boat back instead? The two o'clock ferry, Thursday? I'm sure I'll feel more like it then. All right? What? No, you can't come on deck with me. For God's sake. Besides, I'm going to the lavatory first. I can't have you following me in there, peering round from the next stall.

I apologise; I didn't mean that. Two o'clock, in the bar, as the ferry sails? Oh, and one last word. The cheese shop in the Grande Rue: don't miss it. I think the name's Leroux. I suggest you get a Brillat-Savarin. You won't get a good one in England unless you bring it back yourself. They're kept too cold, or they have chemicals injected into them to delay the ripening, or something. That is, if you like cheese . . .

*　　*　　*　　*　　*

How do we seize the past? How do we seize the foreign past? We read, we learn, we ask, we remember, we are humble; and then a casual detail shifts everything. Flaubert was a giant; they all said so. He towered over everybody like a strapping Gallic chieftain. And yet he was only six feet tall: we have this on his own authority. Tall, but not gigantic; shorter than I am, in fact, and when I am in France I never find myself towering over people like a Gallic chieftain.

So Gustave was a six-foot giant, and the world shrinks just a little with that knowledge. The giants were not so tall (were the dwarfs therefore shorter too?). The fat men: were they less fat because they were smaller, and so you needed less stomach to appear fat; or were they more fat, because they developed the same stomachs, but had even less frame to support them? How can we know such trivial, crucial details? We can study files for decades, but every so often we are tempted to throw up our hands and declare that history is merely another literary genre: the past is autobiographical fiction pretending to be a parliamentary report.

I have a small watercolour of Rouen on my wall by Arthur Frederick Payne (born Newarke, Leicester, 1831, working 1849–84). It shows the city from Bonsecours churchyard: the bridges, the spires, the river bending away past Croisset. It was painted on May 4th, 1856. Flaubert finished *Madame Bovary* on April 30th, 1856: there at Croisset, there where I can jab my finger, between two spreading and unknowing sploshes of watercolour. So near and yet so far. Is this history, then — a swift, confident amateur's watercolour?

I'm not sure what I believe about the past. I just want to know if fat people were fatter then. And were mad people madder? There was a lunatic called Mirabeau in the Rouen asylum who was popular with doctors and medical students at the Hôtel-Dieu because of a particular talent: in exchange for a cup of coffee he would copulate on the dissecting table with a female corpse. (Does the cup of coffee make him more, or less, mad?) One day, however, Mirabeau was to prove a coward: Flaubert reports that he funked his task when faced with a woman who had been guillotined. No doubt they offered him two cups of coffee, extra sugar, a slug of cognac? (And does this prove him saner, or madder, this need for a face, however dead?)

Nowadays we aren't allowed to use the word *mad*. What lunacy. The few psychiatrists I respect always talk about people being mad. Use the short, simple, true words. *Dead*, I say, and *dying*, and *mad*, and *adultery*. I don't say *passed on*, or *slipping away*, or *terminal* (oh, he's terminal? Which one? Euston, St Pancras, the Gare St Lazare?), or *personality disorder*, or *fooling around*, *bit on the side*, *well she's away a lot visiting her sister*. I say *mad* and *adultery*, that's what I say. *Mad* has the right sound to it. It's an ordinary word, a word which tells us how lunacy might come and call like a delivery van. Terrible things are also ordinary. Do you know what Nabokov said about adultery in his lecture on *Madame Bovary*? He said it was 'a most conventional way to rise above the conventional'.

Any history of adultery would doubtless quote Emma's seduction in that careering cab: it's probably the most famous act of infidelity in the whole of nineteenth-century fiction. Easy enough for the reader to imagine such a precisely-described scene, and to get it right, you'd think. Yes indeed. But still easy enough to get it just a tiny bit wrong. I cite G.M. Musgrave, sketcher, traveller, memoirist, and vicar of Borden, Kent: author of *The Parson, Pen and Pencil, or, Reminiscences and Illustrations of an Excursion to Paris, Tours, and Rouen, in the Summer of 1847; with a few Memoranda on French Farming* (Richard Bentley, London, 1848) and of *A Ramble Through Normandy, or, Scenes, Characters and Incidents in a Sketching Excursion Through Calvados* (David Bogue, London, 1855). On page 522 of the latter work the Reverend Musgrave is visiting Rouen — 'the Manchester of France', he calls it — at a time when Flaubert is still flailing away at his *Bovary*. His account of the city includes the following aside:

> I was mentioning, just now, the cab-stand. The carriages stationed there are the most dumpy vehicles, I conceive, of their kind, in Europe. I could with ease place my arm on the roof as I stood by one of them in the road. They are well-built, neat, and cleanly little chariots, with two good lamps; and 'cut' about the streets like Tom Thumb's coach.

So our view suddenly lurches: the famous seduction would have been even more cramped, and even less romantic, than we might previously have assumed. This piece of information is, as far as I am aware, hitherto unrecorded in the extensive annotations which have been inflicted on the novel; and I herewith offer it in a spirit of humility for use by professional scholars.

The tall, the fat, the mad. And then there are the colours. When he was researching for *Madame Bovary*, Flaubert spent a whole afternoon examining the countryside through pieces of coloured glass. Would he have seen what we now see? Presumably. But what about this: in 1853, at Trouville, he watched the sun go down over the sea, and declared that it resembled a large disc of redcurrant jam. Vivid enough. But was redcurrant jam the same colour in Normandy in 1853 as it is now? (Would any pots of it have survived, so that we could check? And how would we know the colour had remained the same in the intervening years?) It's the sort of thing you fret about. I decided to write to the Grocers' Company about the matter. Unlike some of my other correspondents, they replied promptly. They were also reassuring: redcurrant jam is one of the purest jams, they said, and though an 1853 Rouennais pot might not have been quite so clear as a modern one because of the use of unrefined sugar, the colour would have been almost exactly the same. So at least that's all right: now we can go ahead and confidently imagine the sunset. But you see what I mean? (As for my other questions: a pot of the jam could indeed have survived until now, but would almost certainly have turned brown, unless kept completely sealed in a dry, airy, pitch-dark room.)

The Reverend George M. Musgrave was a digressive but observant fellow. He was more than a little inclined to pomposity ('I am bound to speak in terms of high eulogium on the subject of Rouen's literary reputation'), but his fussiness over detail makes him a useful informant. He notes the French love of leeks and the French abhorrence of rain. He interrogates everyone: a Rouen merchant who amazes him by not having heard of mint sauce, and a canon of Evreux who informs him that in France the men read too much, while the women read next to nothing (o rarer still Emma Bovary!). While in Rouen he visits the Cimetière Monumental the year after Gustave's father and sister were buried there, and approves its innovative policy of allowing families to buy freehold plots. Elsewhere, he investigates a fertiliser factory, the Bayeux tapestry, and the lunatic asylum at Caen where Beau Brummell died in 1840 (was Brummell mad? The attendants remembered him well: *un bon enfant*, they said, drank only barley water mixed with a very little wine).

Musgrave also went to the fair at Guibray, and there among the freak shows was The Largest Fat Boy in France: Aimable Jouvin, born at Herblay in 1840, now aged fourteen, admission a penny farthing. How fat was the fat boy? Our rambling sketcher didn't, alas, go in himself and record the young phenomenon with his pencil; but he waited while a French cavalryman paid his penny farthing, entered the caravan, and emerged mouthing 'some very choice Norman phraseology'. Though Musgrave did not bring himself to ask the soldier what he had seen, his impression was 'that

Aimable had not been fattened up to the mark of the visitor's large expectations'.

At Caen Musgrave went to a regatta, where seven thousand spectators lined the dockside. Most of them were men, and most of these were peasants wearing their best blue blouses. The mass effect was of a light but most brilliant ultramarine. It was a particular, exact colour; Musgrave had seen it only once before, in a special department of the Bank of England where they incinerated notes which had been taken out of circulation. Banknote paper was then prepared with a colouring agent made from cobalt, silex, salt and potash: if you set light to a bundle of money, the cinder would take on the extraordinary tint that Musgrave saw on the Caen dockside. The colour of France.

As he travelled on, this colour and its cruder associates became more apparent. The men's blouses and hose were blue; three-quarters of the women's gowns were blue. The horses' housings and collar-decorations were blue; so were the carts, the name-boards of the villages, the agricultural implements, wheelbarrows and water-butts. In many of the towns the houses displayed the cerulean hue, both inside and out. Musgrave found himself compelled to remark to a Frenchman he met that 'There was more *blue* in his country than in any region of the world with which I was acquainted.'

We look at the sun through smoked glass; we must look at the past through coloured glass.

* * * * *

Thank you. *Santé*. You got your cheese, I hope? You won't mind a word of advice? Eat it. Don't put it in a plastic bag in the fridge and save it for visitors; before you know where you are it'll have swollen to three times its size and smell like a chemical factory. You'll open the bag and be putting your face into a bad marriage.

'Giving the public details about oneself is a bourgeois temptation that I have always resisted' (1879). But here goes. You know my name of course: Geoffrey Braithwaite. Don't miss out the l or you'll start turning me into a Parisian grocer. No; just my joke. Look. You know those personal advertisements in magazines like the *New Statesman*? I thought I might do it like that.

> 60+ widowed doctor, children grown up, active, cheerful if
> inclined to melancholy, kindly, non-smoker, amateur Flaubert
> scholar, likes reading, food, travel to familiar places, old films,
> has friends, but seeks . . .

You see the problem. *But seeks* . . . Do I? What do I seek? A tender fortyish div or wid for companionship stroke marriage? No. Mature lady for country walks, occasional dining? No. Bisexual couple for gleesome threesomes? Certainly not. I always read those pining paragraphs in the back of magazines, though I never feel like replying; and I've just realised why. Because I don't believe any of them. They aren't lying — indeed, they're all trying to be utterly sincere — but they aren't telling the truth. The column distorts the way the advertisers describe themselves. No one would think of himself as an active non-smoker inclined to melancholy if that wasn't encouraged, even demanded, by the form. Two conclusions: first, that you can't define yourself directly, just by looking face-on into the mirror; and secondly, that Flaubert was, as always, right. Style does arise from subject-matter. Try as they might, those advertisers are always beaten down by the form; they are forced — even at the one time they need to be candidly personal — into an unwished impersonality.

You can see, at least, the colour of my eyes. Not as complicated as Emma Bovary's, are they? But do they help you? They might mislead. I'm not being coy; I'm trying to be *useful*. Do you know the colour of Flaubert's eyes? No, you don't: for the simple reason that I suppressed it a few pages ago. I didn't want you to be tempted by cheap conclusions. See how carefully I look after you. You don't like it? I *know* you don't like it. All right. Well, according to Du Camp, Gustave the Gallic chieftain, the six-foot giant with a voice like a trumpet, had 'large eyes as grey as the sea'.

I was reading Mauriac the other day: the *Mémoires intérieurs*, written at the very end of his life. It's the time when the final pellets of vanity accumulate into a cyst, when the self starts up its last pathetic murmur of 'Remember me, remember me . . . '; it's the time when the autobiographies get written, the last boasts are made, and the memories which no one else's brain still holds are written down with a false idea of value.

But that's just what Mauriac declines to do. He writes his '*Mémoires*', but they aren't his memoirs. We are spared the counting-games and spelling-bees of childhood, that first servant-girl in the humid attic, the canny uncle with metal teeth and a headful of stories – or whatever. Instead, Mauriac tells us about the books he's read, the painters he's liked, the plays he's seen. He finds himself by looking in the works of others. He defines his own faith by a passionate anger against Gide the Luciferian. Reading his 'memoirs' is like meeting a man on a train who says, 'Don't look at me, that's misleading. If you want to know what I'm like, wait until we're in a tunnel, and then study my reflection in the window.' You wait, and look, and catch a face against a shifting background of sooty walls, cables and sudden brickwork. The transparent shape flickers and jumps, always a few feet away. You become accustomed to its existence, you move with its movements; and though you know its presence is conditional, you feel it to be permanent. Then there is a wail from ahead, a roar and a burst of light; the face is gone for ever.

Well, you know I've got brown eyes; make of that what you will. Six foot one; grey hair; good health. But what matters about me? Only what I know, what I believe, what I can tell you. Nothing much about my character matters. No, that's not true. I'm honest, I'd better tell you that. I'm aiming to tell the truth; though mistakes are, I suppose, inevitable. And if I make them, at least I'm in good company. *The Times*, in its obituary column, May 10th, 1880, claims that Flaubert wrote a book called *Bouvard et Peluchet*, and that he 'at first adopted his father's profession – that of surgeon'. My *Encyclopaedia Britannica*, eleventh edition (the best, they say), suggests that Charles Bovary is a portrait of the novelist's father. The author of this article, a certain 'E.G.', turns out to have been Edmund Gosse. I snorted a bit when I read that. I have a little less time for 'Mr' Gosse since my encounter with Ed Winterton.

I'm honest, I'm reliable. When I was a doctor I never killed a single patient, which is more of a boast than you might imagine. People trusted me; they kept coming back, at any rate. And I was good with the dying. I never got drunk — that is, I never got too drunk; I never wrote prescriptions for imaginary patients; I never made advances to women in my surgery. I sound like a plaster saint. I'm not.

No, I didn't kill my wife. I might have known you'd think that. First you find out that she's dead; then, a while later, I say that I never killed a single patient. Aha, who *did* you kill, then? The question no doubt appears logical. How easy it is to set off speculation. There was a man called Ledoux who maliciously claimed that Flaubert had committed suicide; he wasted a lot of people's time. I'll tell you about him later. But it all goes to prove my point: what knowledge is useful, what knowledge is true? Either I have to give you so much information about myself that you are forced to admit that I could no more have killed my wife than Flaubert could have committed suicide; or else I merely say, That's all, that's enough. No more. *J'y suis, j'y reste*.

I could play the Mauriac game, perhaps. Tell you how I brought myself up on Wells, Huxley and Shaw; how I prefer George Eliot and even Thackeray to Dickens; how I like Orwell, Hardy and Housman, and dislike the Auden–Spender–Isherwood crew (preaching socialism as a sideshoot of homosexual law reform); how I'm saving Virginia Woolf for when I'm dead. The younger fellows? Today's fellows? Well, they each seem to do one thing well enough, but fail to realise that literature depends on doing several things well at the same time. I could go on at great length on all these topics; it would be very pleasant for me to say what I think and relieve Monsieur Geoffrey Braithwaite's feelings by means of such utterances. But what is the importance of the said gentleman?

I'd rather play a different version. Some Italian once wrote that the critic secretly wants to kill the writer. Is that true? Up to a point. We all hate golden eggs. Bloody golden eggs again, you can hear the critics mutter as a good novelist produces yet another good novel; haven't we had enough omelettes this year?

But if not that, then many critics would like to be dictators of literature, to regulate the past, and to set out with quiet authority the future direction of the art. This month, everyone must write about this; next month, nobody is allowed to write about that. So-and-so will not be reprinted until we say so. All copies of this seductively bad novel must be destroyed at once. (You think I am joking? In March 1983, the newspaper *Libération* urged that the French Minister for Women's Rights should put on her Index for 'public provocation to sexist hatred' the following works: *Pantagruel*, *Jude the Obscure*, Baudelaire's poems, all Kafka, *The Snows of Kilimanjaro* — and *Madame Bovary*.) Still, let's play. I'll go first.

1 There shall be no more novels in which a group of people, isolated by circumstances, revert to the 'natural condition' of man, become essential, poor, bare, forked creatures. All that may be written is one short story, the final one of the genre, the cork in the bottle. I'll write it for you. A group of travellers are shipwrecked, or airwrecked, somewhere, no doubt on an island. One of them, a large, powerful, dislikeable man, has a gun. He forces all the others to live in a sandpit of their own digging. Every so often, he takes one of his prisoners out, shoots him or her, and eats the carcass. The food tastes good, and he grows fat. When he has shot and eaten his final prisoner, he begins to worry what he will do for food; but fortunately a seaplane arrives at this point and rescues him. He tells the world that he was the sole survivor of the original wreck, and that he has sustained himself by eating berries, leaves and roots. The world marvels at his fine physical condition, and a poster bearing his photograph is displayed in the windows of vegetarian food shops. He is never found out.

You see how easy it is to write, how much fun it is? That's why I'd ban the genre.

2 There shall be no more novels about incest. No, not even ones in very bad taste.

3 No novels set in abattoirs. This is, I admit, a rather small genre at the moment; but I have recently noticed increasing use of the abattoir in short stories. It must be nipped in the bud.

4 There is to be a twenty-year ban on novels set in Oxford or Cambridge, and a ten-year ban on other university fiction. No ban

on fiction set in polytechnics (though no subsidy to encourage it). No ban on novels set in primary schools; a ten-year ban on secondary-school fiction. A partial ban on growing-up novels (one per author allowed). A partial ban on novels written in the historic present (again, one per author). A total ban on novels in which the main character is a journalist or a television presenter.

5 A quota system is to be introduced on fiction set in South America. The intention is to curb the spread of package-tour baroque and heavy irony. Ah, the propinquity of cheap life and expensive principles, of religion and banditry, of surprising honour and random cruelty. Ah, the daiquiri bird which incubates its eggs on the wing; ah, the fredonna tree whose roots grow at the tips of its branches, and whose fibres assist the hunchback to impregnate by telepathy the haughty wife of the hacienda owner; ah, the opera house now overgrown by jungle. Permit me to rap on the table and murmur 'Pass!' Novels set in the Arctic and the Antarctic will receive a development grant.

6a No scenes in which carnal connection takes place between a human being and an animal. The woman and the porpoise, for instance, whose tender coupling symbolises a wider mending of those gossamer threads which formerly bound the world together in peaceable companionship. No, none of that.

b No scenes in which carnal connection takes place between man and woman (porpoise-like, you might say) in the shower. My reasons are primarily aesthetic, but also medical.

7 No novels about small, hitherto forgotten wars in distant parts of the British Empire, in the painstaking course of which we learn first, that the British are averagely wicked; and secondly, that war is very nasty indeed.

8 No novels in which the narrator, or any of the characters, is identified simply by an initial letter. Still they go on doing it!

9 There shall be no more novels which are really about other novels. No 'modern versions', reworkings, sequels or prequels. No imaginative completions of works left unfinished on their author's death. Instead, every writer is to be issued with a sampler in coloured wools to hang over the fireplace. It reads: Knit Your Own Stuff.

10 There shall be a twenty-year ban on God; or rather, on the allegorical, metaphorical, allusive, offstage, imprecise and ambiguous uses of God. The bearded head gardener who is always tending the apple tree; the wise old sea-captain who never rushes to judgment; the character you're not quite introduced to, but who is giving you a creepy feeling by Chapter Four . . . pack them off into storage, all of them. God is permitted only as a verifiable divinity who gets extremely cross at man's transgressions.

So how do we seize the past? As it recedes, does it come into focus? Some think so. We know more, we discover extra documents, we use infra-red light to pierce erasures in the correspondence, and we are free of contemporary prejudice; so we understand better. Is that it? I wonder. Take Gustave's sex-life. For years it was assumed that the bear of Croisset broke out of his bearishness solely with Louise Colet — 'the only sentimental episode of any importance in the life of Flaubert,' Emile Faguet declared. But then Elisa Schlesinger is discovered — the bricked-up royal chamber in Gustave's heart, the slow-burning fire, the adolescent passion never consummated. Next, more letters come into view, and the Egyptian journals. The life begins to reek of actresses; the bedding of Bouilhet is announced; Flaubert himself admits a taste for Cairo bath-house boys. At last we see the whole shape of his carnality; he is ambi-sexual, omni-experienced.

But not so fast. Sartre decrees that Gustave was never homosexual; merely passive and feminine in his psychology. The byplay with Bouilhet was just teasing, the outer edge of vivid male friendship: Gustave never committed a single homosexual act in all his life. He says he did, but that was boastful invention: Bouilhet asked for salacities from Cairo, and Flaubert provided them. (Are we convinced by this? Sartre accuses Flaubert of wishful thinking. Might we not accuse Sartre of the same? Wouldn't he prefer Flaubert the trembling bourgeois, joking on the edge of a sin he fears to commit, rather than Flaubert the daredevil, the subversive indulger?) And in the meantime, we are also being encouraged to shift our view of Mme Schlesinger. Current belief among Flaubert-istes is that the relationship was consummated after all: either in 1848 or, more probably, in the early months of 1843.

The past is a distant, receding coastline, and we are all in the same boat. Along the stern rail there is a line of telescopes; each brings the shore into focus at a given distance. If the boat is becalmed, one of the telescopes will be in continual use; it will seem to tell the whole, the unchanging truth. But this is an illusion; and as the boat sets off again, we return to our normal activity: scurrying from one telescope to another, seeing the sharpness fade in one, waiting for the blur to clear in another. And when the blur does clear, we imagine that we have made it do so all by ourselves.

Isn't the sea calmer than the other day? And heading north — the light that Boudin saw. What does this journey seem like to those who aren't British — as they head towards the land of embarrassment and breakfast? Do they make nervous jokes about fog and porridge? Flaubert found London scaring; it was an unhealthy city, he declared, where it was impossible to find a *pot-au-feu*. On the other hand, Britain was the home of Shakespeare, clear thinking and political liberty, the land where Voltaire had been welcomed and to which Zola would flee.

Now what is it? First slum of Europe, one of our poets called it not long ago. First hypermarket of Europe might be more like it. Voltaire praised our attitude to commerce, and the lack of snobbery which allowed the younger sons of the gentry to become businessmen. Now the day-trippers arrive from Holland and Belgium, Germany and France, excited about the weakness of the pound and eager to get into Marks & Spencer. Commerce, Voltaire declared, was the base on which the greatness of our nation was built; now it's all that keeps us from going bankrupt.

When I drive off the boat, I always have a desire to go through the Red Channel. I never have more than the permitted amount of duty-free goods; I've never imported plants, or dogs, or drugs, or uncooked meat, or firearms; and yet I constantly find myself wanting to turn the wheel and head for the Red Channel. It always feels like an admission of failure to come back from the Continent and have nothing to show for it. Would you read this, please, sir? Yes. Have you understood it, sir? Yes. Have you anything to declare? Yes, I'd like to declare a small case of French flu, a dangerous fondness for Flaubert, a childish delight in French road-signs, and a love of the light as you look north. Is there any duty to pay on any of these? There ought to be.

Oh, and I've got this cheese, too. A Brillat-Savarin. That fellow behind me has got one too. I told him you always had to declare your cheese at customs. Say cheese.

I hope you don't think I'm being enigmatic, by the way. If I'm irritating, it's probably because I'm embarrassed; I told you I don't like the full face. But I really am trying to make things easier for you. Mystification is simple; clarity is the hardest thing of all. Not writing a tune is easier than writing one. Not rhyming is easier than rhyming. I don't mean art should be as clear as the instructions on a packet of seeds; I'm saying that you trust the mystifier more if you know he's deliberately choosing not to be lucid. You trust Picasso all the way because he could draw like Ingres.

But what helps? What do we need to know? Not everything. Everything confuses. Directness also confuses. The full-face portrait staring back at you hypnotises. Flaubert is usually looking away in his portraits and photographs. He's looking away so that you can't catch his eye; he's also looking away because what he can see over your shoulder is more interesting than your shoulder.

Directness confuses. I told you my name: Geoffrey Braithwaite. Has that helped? A little; at least it's better than 'B' or 'G' or 'the man' or 'the amateur of cheeses'. And if you hadn't seen me, what would you have deduced from the name? Middle-class professional man; solicitor perhaps; denizen of pine-and-heather country; pepper-and-salt tweeds; a moustache hinting – perhaps fraudulently – at a military past; a sensible wife; perhaps a little boating at weekends; more of a gin than a whisky man; and so on?

I am – was – a doctor, first-generation professional class; as you see, there's no moustache, though I have the military past which men of my age couldn't avoid; I live in Essex, most characterless and therefore most acceptable of the Home Counties; whisky, not gin; no tweed at all; and no boating. Near enough, and yet not near enough, you see. As for my wife, she was not sensible. That was one of the last words anyone would apply to her. They inject soft cheeses, as I said, to stop them ripening too quickly. But they always do ripen; it's in their nature. Soft cheeses collapse; firm cheeses indurate. Both go mouldy.

I was going to put my photograph in the front of the book. Not vanity; just trying to be helpful. But I'm afraid it was rather an old photograph; taken about ten years ago. I haven't got a more recent one. That's something you find: after a certain age, people stop photographing you. Or rather, they photograph you only on formal occasions: birthdays, weddings, Christmas. A flushed and jolly character raises his glass among friends and family — how real, how reliable is *that* evidence? What would the photos of my twenty-fifth wedding anniversary have revealed? Certainly not the truth; so perhaps it's as well they were never taken.

Flaubert's niece Caroline says that towards the end of his life he regretted not having had a wife and family. Her account is, however, rather spare. The two of them were walking by the Seine after a visit to some friends. '"They got it right," he said to me, alluding to that household with its charming and honest children. "Yes," he repeated to himself gravely, "they got it right." I did not trouble his thoughts, but remained silent at his side. This walk was one of our last.'

I rather wish she *had* troubled his thoughts. Did he really mean it? Should we take the remark as more than the reflex perversity of a man who dreamed of Egypt while in Normandy, and of Normandy while in Egypt? Was he doing more than praise the particular talents of the family they had just visited? After all, had he wanted to praise the institution of marriage itself, he could have turned to his niece and regretted his solitary life by admitting, '*You* got it right.' But he didn't, of course; because she got it wrong. She married a weakling who turned into a bankrupt, and in helping save her husband she bankrupted her uncle. The case of Caroline is instructive — gloomily so to Flaubert.

Her own father had been as much of a weakling as her husband subsequently became; Gustave supplanted him. In her *Souvenirs intimes* Caroline recalls her uncle's return from Egypt when she was a small girl: he arrives home unexpectedly one evening, wakes her, picks her up out of bed, bursts out laughing because her nightdress extends far below her feet, and plants great kisses on her cheeks. He has just come from outdoors: his moustache is cold, and damp with dew. She is frightened, and much relieved when he puts her down. What is this but a textbook account of the absent father's alarming return to the household — the return from the war, from business, from abroad, from philandering, from danger?

He adored her. In London he carried her round the Great Exhibition; this time she was happy to be in his arms, safe from the frightening crowds. He taught her history: the story of Pelopidas and Epaminondas; he taught her geography, taking a shovel and pail of water into the garden, where he would build for her instructive peninsulas, islands, gulfs and promontories. She loved her childhood with him, and the memory of it survived the misfortunes of her adult life. In 1930, when she was eighty-four, Caroline met Willa Cather in Aix-les-Bains, and recalled the hours spent eighty years earlier on a rug in the corner of Gustave's study: he working, she reading, in strict but proudly observed silence. 'She liked to think, as she lay in her corner, that she was shut in a cage with some powerful wild animal, a tiger or a lion or a bear, who had devoured his keeper and would spring upon anyone else who opened his door, but with whom she was "quite safe and conceited", as she said with a chuckle.'

But then the necessities of adulthood arrived. He advised her badly, and she married a weakling. She became a snob; she thought only of smart society; and finally she tried to turn her uncle out of the very house in which the most useful things she knew had been inserted into her brain.

Epaminondas was a Theban general, held to be living proof of all the virtues; he led a career of principled carnage, and founded the city of Megalopolis. As he lay dying, one of those present lamented his lack of issue. He replied, 'I leave two children, Leuctra and Mantinea' — the sites of his two most famous victories. Flaubert might have made a similar avowal — 'I leave two children, Bouvard and Pécuchet' — because his only child, the niece who became a daughter, had departed into disapproving adulthood. To her, and to her husband, he had become 'the consumer'.

Gustave taught Caroline about literature. I quote her: 'He considered no book dangerous that was well written.' Move forward seventy years or so to a different household in another part of France. This time there is a bookish boy, a mother, and a friend of the mother's called Mme Picard. The boy later wrote his memoirs; again, I quote: 'Mme Picard's opinion was that a child should be allowed to read everything. "No book can be dangerous if it is well written".' The boy, aware of Mme Picard's frequently expressed view, deliberately exploits her presence and asks his mother's permission to read a particular and notorious novel. 'But if my little darling reads books like that at his age,' says the mother, 'what will he do when he grows up?' 'I shall live them out!' he replies. It was one of the cleverest retorts of his childhood; it went down in family history, and it won him — or so we are left to assume — readership of the novel. The boy was Jean-Paul Sartre. The book was *Madame Bovary*.

Does the world progress? Or does it merely shuttle back and forth like a ferry? An hour from the English coast and the clear sky disappears. Cloud and rain escort you back to where you belong. As the weather changes, the boat begins to roll a little, and the tables in the bar resume their metallic conversation. *Rattarattarattaratta*, *fattafattafattafatta*. Call and response, call and response. Now it sounds to me like the final stages of a marriage: two separated parties, screwed to their own particular pieces of floor, uttering routine chatter while the rain begins to fall. My wife ... Not now, not now.

Pécuchet, during his geological investigations, speculates on what would happen if there were an earthquake beneath the English Channel. The water, he concludes, would rush out into the Atlantic; the coasts of England and France would totter, shift and reunite; the Channel would cease to exist. On hearing his friend's predictions, Bouvard runs away in terror. For myself, I do not think we need to be quite so pessimistic.

You won't forget about the cheese, will you? Don't grow a

chemical plant in your fridge. I didn't ask if you were married. My compliments, or not, as the case may be.

I think I shall go through the Red Channel this time. I feel the need for some company. The Reverend Musgrave's opinion was that French *douaniers* behaved like gentlemen, while English customs officers were ruffians. But I find them all quite sympathetic, if you treat them properly.

8

The Train-spotter's Guide to Flaubert

1 The house at Croisset — a long, white, eighteenth-century property on the banks of the Seine — was perfect for Flaubert. It was isolated, yet close to Rouen and thence to Paris. It was large enough for him to have a grand study with five windows; yet small enough for him to discourage visitors without obvious discourtesy. It gave him, too, if he wanted it, an unthreatened view of passing life: from the terrace he could train his opera glasses on the pleasure-steamers taking Sunday lunchers to La Bouille. For their part, the lunchers grew accustomed to *cet original de Monsieur Flaubert*, and were disappointed if they didn't spot him, in Nubian shirt and silk skullcap, gazing back at them, taking the novelist's view.

Caroline has described the quiet evenings of her childhood at Croisset. It was a curious *ménage*: the girl, the uncle, the grand-mother — a solitary representative of each generation, like one of those squeezed houses you sometimes see with a single room on each storey. (The French call such a house *un bâton de perroquet*, a parrot's perch.) The three of them, she recalled, would often sit at the balcony of the little pavilion and watch the confident arrival of the night. On the far bank they might just discern the silhouette of a straining horse on the tow-path; from nearby they might just hear a discreet splosh as the eel-fishermen cast off and slipped out into the stream.

Why did Dr Flaubert sell his property at Déville to buy this house?

Traditionally, as a refuge for his invalid son, who had just suffered his first attack of epilepsy. But the property at Déville would have been sold anyway. The Paris to Rouen railway was being extended to Le Havre, and the line cut straight through Dr Flaubert's land; part of it was to be compulsorily purchased. You could say that Gustave was shepherded into creative retreat at Croisset by epilepsy. You could also say he was driven there by the railway.

2 Gustave belonged to the first railway generation in France; and he hated the invention. For a start, it was an odious means of transport. 'I get so fed up on a train that after five minutes I'm howling with boredom. Passengers think it's a neglected dog; not at all, it's M. Flaubert, sighing.' Secondly, it produced a new figure at the dinner table: the railway bore. Conversation on the topic gave Flaubert a *colique des wagons*; in June 1843 he pronounced the railways to be the third most boring subject imaginable after Mme Lafarge (an arsenic poisoner) and the death of the Duc d'Orleans (killed in his carriage the previous year). Louise Colet, striving for modernity in her poem 'La Paysanne', allowed Jean, her soldier returning from the wars in search of his Jeanneton, to notice the running smoke of a train. Flaubert cut the line. 'Jean doesn't give a damn about that sort of thing,' he growled, 'and nor do I.'

But he didn't just hate the railway as such; he hated the way it flattered people with the illusion of progress. What was the point of scientific advance without moral advance? The railway would merely permit more people to move about, meet and be stupid together. In one of his earliest letters, written when he was fifteen, he lists the misdeeds of modern civilisation: 'Railways, poisons, enema pumps, cream tarts, royalty and the guillotine.' Two years later, in his essay on Rabelais, the list of enemies has altered — all except the first item: 'Railways, factories, chemists and mathematicians.' He never changed.

3 'Superior to everything is — Art. A book of poetry is preferable to a railway.'

Intimate Notebook, 1840

4 The function of the railway in Flaubert's affair with Louise Colet
has, to my mind, been rather underestimated. Consider the mechan-
ics of their relationship. She lived in Paris, he at Croisset; he
wouldn't come to the capital, she wasn't allowed to visit him in the
country. So they would meet approximately half-way, at Mantes,
where the Hôtel du Grand Cerf would allow them a night or two of
lurid rapture and false promises. Afterwards, the following cycle
would take place: Louise would assume an early rendezvous;
Gustave would put her off; Louise would plead, grow angry,
threaten; Gustave would reluctantly give in and agree to another
meeting. It would last just long enough to sate his desires and
rekindle her expectations. And so this grumbling three-legged race
was run. Did Gustave ever reflect on the fate of an earlier visitor to
the town? It was at the capture of Mantes that William the Con-
queror fell from his horse and received the injury from which he later
died in Rouen.

   The Paris to Rouen railway — built by the English — opened on
May 9th, 1843, barely three years before Gustave and Louise met.
The journey to Mantes, for each of them, was cut from a day to a
couple of hours. Imagine what it would have been like without the
railway. They would have travelled by diligence or river-steamer;
they would have been tired and perhaps irritable on seeing one
another again. Fatigue affects desire. But in view of the difficulties,
more would have been expected of the occasion: more in time — an
extra day perhaps — and more in emotional commitment. This is
just my theory, of course. But if the telephone in our century has
made adultery both simpler and harder (assignations are easier, but
so is checking up), the railway in the last century had a similar
effect. (Has anyone made a comparative study of the spread of
railways and the spread of adultery? I can imagine village priests
delivering sermons on the Devil's invention and being mocked for it;
but if they did, they were right.) The railway made it worth while
for Gustave: he could get to Mantes and back without too much
trouble; and Louise's complaints perhaps seemed a reasonable price
to pay for such accessible pleasure. The railway made it worth while
for Louise: Gustave was never really far away, however severe he

sounded in his letters; the next one would surely say that they could meet again, that only two hours separated them. And the railway made it worth while for us, who can now read the letters which resulted from that prolonged erotic oscillation.

5 a) September 1846: the first meeting at Mantes. The only problem was Gustave's mother. She had not as yet been officially informed of Louise's existence. Indeed, Mme Colet was obliged to send all her love letters to Gustave via Maxime du Camp, who then readdressed them in fresh envelopes. How would Mme Flaubert react to Gustave's sudden nocturnal absence? What could he tell her? A lie, of course: 'une petite histoire que ma mère a crue,' he boasted, like a proud six-year-old, and set off for Mantes.

But Mme Flaubert didn't believe his petite histoire. She slept less that night than Gustave and Louise did. Something had made her uneasy; perhaps the recent cascade of letters from Maxime du Camp. So the next morning she went to Rouen station, and when her son, still wearing a fresh crust of pride and sex, got off the train, she was waiting for him on the platform. 'She didn't utter any reproach, but her face was the greatest reproach anyone could make.'

They talk about the sadness of departure; what about the guilt of arrival?

b) Louise, of course, could play the platform scene as well. Her habit of jealously bursting in on Gustave when he was dining with friends was notorious. She always expected to find a rival; but there was no rival, unless you count Emma Bovary. On one occasion, Du Camp records, 'Flaubert was leaving Paris for Rouen when she entered the waiting-room of the station and went through such tragic scenes that the railway officials were obliged to interfere. Flaubert was distressed and begged for mercy, but she gave him no quarter.'

6 It is a little-known fact that Flaubert travelled on the London Underground. I quote items from his skeleton travel diary of 1866:

Monday 26 June (on the train from Newhaven). A few insigni-

ficant stations with posters, just as at stations on the outskirts of
Paris. Arrival at Victoria.

Monday 3 July. Bought a railway timetable.

Friday 7 July. Underground railway – Hornsey. Mrs Farmer . . .
To Charing Cross station for information.

He does not deign to compare the British and the French railways.
This is perhaps a pity. Our friend the Reverend G. M. Musgrave,
disembarking at Boulogne a dozen years earlier, was much
impressed by the French system: 'The contrivances for receiving,
weighing, marking and paying for luggage were simple and
excellent. Regularity, precision, and punctuality did the work well
in every department. Much civility, much comfort (comfort in
France!) made every arrangement pleasurable; and all this without
more vociferation or commotion than prevails at Paddington; to say
nothing of the second-class carriage being nearly equal to our first.
Shame to England that it should be thus!'

7 'RAILWAYS: If Napoleon had had them at his disposition, he would
have been invincible. Always go into ecstasies about their invention,
and say: "I, Monsieur, I who am even now speaking to you, was
only this morning at X . . . ; I left by the X-o'clock train; I did the
business I had to do there; and by X-o'clock I was back."'

Dictionnaire de idées reçues

8 I took the train from Rouen (Rive Droite). There were blue plastic
seats and a warning in four languages not to lean out of the window;
English, I noticed, requires more words than French, German or
Italian to convey this advice. I sat beneath a metal-framed photograph (black and white) of fishing-boats at the Île d'Oléron. Next to
me an elderly couple were reading a story in *Paris-Normandie* about a
charcutier, *fou d'amour*, who had killed a family of seven. On the
window was a small sticker I hadn't seen before: '*Ne jetez pas l'énergie
par les fenêtres en les ouvrant en période de chauffage.*' Do not throw
energy out of the windows – How unEnglish the phrasing was;
logical yet fanciful at the same time.

I was being observant, you see. A single ticket costs 35 francs. The journey takes a minute or so under the hour: half what it took in Flaubert's day. Oissel is the first stop; then Le Vaudreuil — *ville nouvelle*; Gaillon (Aubevoye), with its Grand Marnier warehouse. Musgrave suggested the scenery along this stretch of the Seine reminded him of Norfolk: 'more like English scenery than any district I had seen in Europe.' The ticket-collector raps on the door-jamb with his punch: metal on metal, an order you obey. Vernon; then, on your left, the broad Seine conducts you into Mantes.

6, place de la République was a building site. A square block of flats was almost finished; already it exhibited the confident innocence of the usurper. The Grand Cerf? Yes, indeed, they told me at the *tabac*, the old building had stood until a year or so ago. I went back and stared again. All that now remained of the Hôtel was a couple of tall stone gateposts some thirty feet apart. I gazed at them hopelessly. On the train, I had been unable to imagine Flaubert (howling like an impatient dog? grumbling? ardent?) making the same journey; now at this point of pilgrimage, the gateposts were no help in thinking my way back to the hot reunions of Gustave and Louise. Why should they be? We are too impertinent with the past, counting on it in this way for a reliable *frisson*. Why should it play our game?

Grumpily I circled the church (Michelin one star), bought a newspaper, drank a cup of coffee, read about the charcutier, *fou d'amour*, and decided to take the next train back. The road leading to the station is called avenue Franklin Roosevelt, though the reality is a little less grand than the name. Fifty yards from the end, on the left, I came across a café-restaurant. It was called Le Perroquet. Outside, on the pavement, a fretworked wooden parrot with garish green plumage was holding the lunch menu in its beak. The building had one of those brightly timbered exteriors which assert more age than they probably possess. I don't know if it would have been there in Flaubert's day. But I know this. Sometimes the past may be a greased pig; sometimes a bear in its den; and sometimes merely the flash of a parrot, two mocking eyes that spark at you from the forest.

9 Trains play little part in Flaubert's fiction. This shows accuracy, however, not prejudice: most of his work is set before the English navvies and engineers descended on Normandy. *Bouvard et Pécuchet* pokes over into the railway age, but neither of his opinionated copyists, perhaps surprisingly, has a published view on the new mode of transport.

Trains occur only in *L'Education sentimentale*. They are first mentioned as a not very arresting topic of conversation at a soirée given by the Dambreuses. The first real train, and the first real journey, occur in Part Two, chapter three, when Frédéric goes to Creil in the hope of seducing Mme Arnoux. Given the benign impatience of his traveller, Flaubert informs the excursion with an approving lyricism: green plains, stations slipping by like little stage sets, fleecy smoke from the engine dancing briefly on the grass before dispersing. There are several more railway journeys in the novel, and the passengers seem happy enough; at least, none of them howls with boredom like a neglected dog. And though Flaubert aggressively excised from 'La Paysanne' Mme Colet's line about the running smoke on the horizon, this doesn't debar from his own countryside (Part Three, chapter four) 'the smoke of a railway engine stretching out in a horizontal line, like a gigantic ostrich feather whose tip kept blowing away.'

We may detect his private opinion only at one point. Pellerin, the artist among Frédéric's companions, a man who specialises in complete theories and incomplete sketches, produces one of his rare finished paintings. Flaubert allows himself a private smile: 'It represented the Republic, or Progress, or Civilisation, in the figure of Jesus Christ, driving a locomotive through a virgin forest.'

10 The penultimate sentence of Gustave's life, uttered as he stood feeling dizzy but not at all alarmed: 'I think I'm going to have a kind of fainting fit. It's lucky it should happen today; it would have been a great nuisance tomorrow, in the train.'

11 At the buffers. Croisset today. The vast paper factory was churning away on the site of Flaubert's house. I wandered inside; they were happy to show me round. I gazed at the pistons, the steam, the

vats and the slopping trays: so much wetness to produce something as dry as paper. I asked my guide if they made the sort of paper that was used for books; she said they made every sort of paper. The tour, I realised, would not prove sentimental. Above our heads a huge drum of paper, some twenty feet wide, was slowly tracking along on a conveyor. It seemed out of proportion to its surroundings, like a piece of pop sculpture on a deliberately provoking scale. I remarked that it resembled a gigantic roll of lavatory paper; my guide confirmed that this was exactly what it was.

Outside the thumping factory things were scarcely quieter. Lorries bullied past on the road that had once been a tow-path; pile-drivers banged on both sides of the river; no boat could pass without hooting. Flaubert used to claim that Pascal had once visited the house at Croisset; and a tenacious local legend maintained that Abbé Prévost wrote *Manon Lescaut* there. Nowadays there is no one left to repeat such fictions; and no one to believe them either.

A sullen Normandy rain was falling. I thought of the horse's silhouette on the far bank, and the quiet splosh as the eel-fishermen cast off. Could even eels live in this cheerless commercial conduit? If they did, they would probably taste of diesel and detergent. My eye moved upriver, and suddenly I noticed it, squat and shuddering. A train. I'd seen the rails before, a set laid between the road and the water; the rain was now making them glisten and smirk. I'd assumed without thinking that they were for the straddling dock cranes to run on. But no: he hasn't even been spared this. The swaddled goods train was drawn up about two hundred yards away, ready to make its run past Flaubert's pavilion. It would doubtless hoot derisively as it drew level; perhaps it was carrying poisons, enema pumps and cream tarts, or supplies for chemists and mathematicians. I didn't want to see the event (irony can be heavy-handed as well as ruthless). I climbed into my car and drove off.

9

The Flaubert Apocrypha

> *It is not what they built. It is what they knocked down.*
> *It is not the houses. It is the spaces between the houses.*
> *It is not the streets that exist. It is the streets*
> *that no longer exist.*

But it's also what they didn't build. It's the houses they dreamed and sketched. It's the brusque boulevards of the imagination; it's that untaken, sauntering path between toupeed cottages; it's the *trompe-l'oeil* cul-de-sac which bluffs you into the belief that you're entering some smart avenue.

Do the books that writers don't write matter? It's easy to forget them, to assume that the apocryphal bibliography must contain nothing but bad ideas, justly abandoned projects, embarrassing first thoughts. It needn't be so: first thoughts are often best, cheeringly rehabilitated by third thoughts after they've been loured at by seconds. Besides, an idea isn't always abandoned because it fails some quality control test. The imagination doesn't crop annually like a reliable fruit tree. The writer has to gather whatever's there: sometimes too much, sometimes too little, sometimes nothing at all. And in the years of glut there is always a slatted wooden tray in some cool, dark attic, which the writer nervously visits from time to time; and yes, oh dear, while he's been hard at work downstairs, up in the attic there are puckering skins, warning spots, a sudden brown collapse and the sprouting of snowflakes. What can he do about it?

With Flaubert, the apocrypha cast a second shadow. If the sweetest moment in life is a visit to the brothel which doesn't come off, perhaps the sweetest moment in writing is the arrival of that idea for a book which never has to be written, which is never sullied with a definite shape, which never needs be exposed to a less loving gaze than that of its author.

Of course, the published works themselves aren't immutable: they might now look different had Flaubert been awarded time and money to put his literary estate in order. *Bouvard et Pécuchet* would have been finished; *Madame Bovary* might have been suppressed (how seriously do we take Gustave's petulance against the overbearing fame of the book? a little seriously); and *L'Education sentimentale* might have had a different ending. Du Camp records his friend's dismay at the book's historical misfortune: a year after publication came the Franco-Prussian war, and it seemed to Gustave that the invasion and the débâcle at Sedan would have provided a grand, public and irrebuttable conclusion to a novel which set out to trace the moral failure of a generation.

'Imagine', Du Camp reports him as saying, 'the capital one might have made out of certain incidents. Here, for instance, is one which would have been excellent in calibre. The capitulation has been signed, the army is under arrest, the Emperor, sunk back in a corner of his large carriage, is gloomy and dull-eyed; he smokes a cigarette to keep himself in countenance, and though a tempest is raging within him, tries to appear impassive. Beside him are his aides-de-camp and a Prussian General. All are silent, each glance is lowered; there is pain in every heart.

'Where the two roads cross the procession is stopped by a column of prisoners guarded by some Uhlans, who wear the chapska perched on their ear, and ride with couched lances. The carriage has to be stopped before the human flood, which advances amid a cloud of dust, reddened by the rays of the sun. The men walk dragging their feet and with slouched shoulders. The Emperor's languid eye contemplates this crowd. What a strange way to review his troops. He thinks of previous reviews, of the drums beating, of the waving standards, of his generals covered with gold lace and saluting him with their swords, and of his guard shouting, "Vive l'Empereur!"

'A prisoner recognises him and salutes him, then another and another.

'Suddenly a Zouave leaves the ranks, shakes his fist and cries, "Ah! There you are, you villain; we have been ruined by you!"

'Then ten thousand men yell insults, wave their arms threateningly, spit upon the carriage, and pass like a whirlwind of curses. The Emperor still remains immovable without making a sign or uttering a word, but, he thinks, "Those are the men they used to call my Praetorian Guards!"

'Well, what do you think of that for a situation? It is pretty powerful, is it not? That would have made rather a stirring final scene for my *Education*? I cannot console myself for having missed it.'

Should we mourn such a lost ending? And how do we assess it? Du Camp probably coarsened it in the retelling, and there would have been many Flaubertian redraftings before publication. Its appeal is clear: the *fortissimo* climax, the public conclusion to a nation's private failing. But does the book need such an ending? Having had 1848, do we need 1870 as well? Better to let the novel die away in disenchantment; better the downbeat reminiscing of two friends than a swirling salon-picture.

For the Apocrypha proper, let us be systematic.

1 *Autobiography*. 'One day, if I write my memoirs – the only thing I shall write well, if ever I put myself to the task of doing it – you will find a place in them, and what a place! For you have blown a large breach in the walls of my existence.' Gustave writes this in one of his earliest letters to Louise Colet; and over a seven-year period (1846–53) he makes occasional references to the planned autobiography. Then he announces its official abandonment. But was it ever more than just a project for a project? 'I'll put you in my memoirs' is one of the handier clichés of literary wooing. File it alongside 'I'll put you in motion pictures', 'I could immortalise you in paint', 'I can just see your neck in marble', etc, etc.

2 *Translations*. Lost works, rather than strict apocrypha; but we might note here: a) Juliet Herbert's translation of *Madame Bovary*, which the novelist oversaw, and which he proclaimed 'a masterpiece'; b) the translation referred to in a letter of 1844: 'I have read

Candide twenty times. I have translated it into English . . .' This does not sound like a school exercise: more like a piece of self-imposed apprenticeship. Judging from Gustave's erratic use of English in his letters, the translation probably added a layer of unintentional comedy to the intentions of the original. He couldn't even copy English place-names accurately: in 1866, making notes on the 'coloured Minton tiles' at the South Kensington Museum, he turns Stoke-upon-Trent into 'Stroke-upon-Trend'.

3 *Fiction*. This section of the Apocrypha contains a large amount of juvenilia, useful mainly to the psychobiographer. But the books a writer fails to write in his adolescence are of a different nature from the books he fails to write once he has announced his profession. These are the not-books for which he must take responsibility.

In 1850, while in Egypt, Flaubert spends two days pondering the story of Mycerinus, a pious king of the fourth dynasty who is credited with reopening temples closed by his predecessors. In a letter to Bouilhet, however, the novelist characterises his subject more crudely as 'the king who fucks his daughter'. Perhaps Flaubert's interest was encouraged by the discovery (or indeed the memory) that in 1837 the king's sarcophagus had been excavated by the British and shipped back to London. Gustave would have been able to inspect it when he visited the British Museum in 1851.

I tried to inspect it myself the other day. The sarcophagus, they told me, is not one of the Museum's more interesting possessions, and hasn't been on display since 1904. Though believed to be fourth dynasty when it was shipped, it later turned out to be twenty-sixth dynasty: the portions of mummified body inside might, or equally might not, be those of Mycerinus. I felt disappointed, but also relieved: what if Flaubert had continued with his project, and inserted a meticulously-researched description of the king's tomb? Dr Enid Starkie would have been given the chance to swat another Mistake in Literature.

(Perhaps I should award Dr Starkie an entry in my pocket guide to Flaubert; or would that be unnecessarily vindictive? S for Sade, or S for Starkie? It's coming along well, by the way, Braithwaite's Dictionary of Accepted Ideas. All you need to know about Flaubert to know as much as the next person! Only a few more entries and I'll be finished. The letter X is going to be a problem, I can see. There's nothing under X in Flaubert's own Dictionary.)

In 1850, from Constantinople, Flaubert announces three projects: 'Une nuit de Don Juan' (which reaches the planning stage); 'Anubis', the story of 'the woman who wants to be fucked by a god'; and 'My Flemish novel about the young girl who dies a virgin and a mystic ... in a little provincial town, at the bottom of a garden planted with cabbages and bulrushes ... ' Gustave complains in this letter to Bouilhet about the dangers of planning a project too thoroughly: 'It seems to me, alas, that if you can so thoroughly dissect your children who are still to be born, you don't get horny enough actually to father them.' In the present cases, Gustave didn't get horny enough; though some see in his third project a vague forerunner of either *Madame Bovary* or *Un cœur simple*.

In 1852-3 Gustave makes serious plans for 'La Spirale', a 'grand, metaphysical, fantastical and bawling novel', whose hero lives a typically Flaubertian double life, being happy in his dreams and unhappy in his real life. Its conclusion, of course: that happiness exists only in the imagination.

In 1853, 'one of my old dreams' is resuscitated: a novel about chivalry. Despite Ariosto such a project is still feasible, Gustave declares: the additional elements he will bring to the subject are 'terror and a broader poetry'.

In 1861: 'I've long been meditating a novel on insanity, or rather on how one becomes insane.' From about this time, or a little later, he was also meditating, according to Du Camp, a novel about the theatre; he would sit in the green room jotting down the confidences of over-candid actresses. 'Only Le Sage in *Gil Blas* has touched upon the truth. I will reveal it in all its nakedness, for it is impossible to imagine how comic it is.'

From this point on, Flaubert must have known that any full-length novel would probably take him five to seven years; and therefore that most of his back-burner projects would inevitably boil themselves dry in the pot. From the last dozen years of his life we find four main ideas, plus an intriguing fifth, a sort of *roman trouvé*.

a) 'Harel-Bey', an Eastern story. 'If I were younger and had the money, I'd go back to the Orient — to study the modern Orient, the Orient of the Isthmus of Suez. A big book about that is one of my old dreams. I'd like to show a civilised man who turns barbarian, and a barbarian who becomes a civilised man — to develop that contrast between two worlds that end up merging . . . But it's too late.'

b) A book about the Battle of Thermopylae, which he planned to write after finishing *Bouvard et Pécuchet*.

c) A novel featuring several generations of a Rouen family.

d) If you cut a flatworm in half, the head will grow a new tail; more surprisingly, the tail will grow a new head. This is what happened with the regretted ending to *L'Education sentimentale*: it generated an entire novel of its own, called first 'Under Napoleon III', and later 'A Parisian Household'. 'I will write a novel about the Empire [Du Camp reports him saying] and bring in the evening receptions at Compiègne, with all the ambassadors, marshals and senators rattling their decorations as they bend to the ground to kiss the hand of the Prince Imperial. Yes indeed! The period will furnish material for some capital books.'

e) The *roman trouvé* was found by Charles Lapierre, editor of *Le Nouvelliste de Rouen*. Dining at Croisset one evening, Lapierre told Flaubert the scandalous history of Mademoiselle de P—. She had been born into the Normandy nobility, had connections at Court, and was appointed reader to the Empress Eugénie. Her beauty, they said, was enough to damn a saint. It was certainly enough to damn her: an open liaison with an officer of the Imperial Guard caused her dismissal. Subsequently she became one of the queens of the Parisian demi-monde, ruling in the late 1860s over a loucher version of the Court from which she had been excluded. During the Franco-Prussian War, she disappeared from sight (along with the rest of her profession), and afterwards her star waned. She descended, by all accounts, to the lowest levels of harlotry. And yet, encouragingly (for fiction as well as for herself), she proved able to rise again: she became the established mistress of a cavalry officer, and by the time she died was the legal wife of an admiral.

Flaubert was delighted with the story: 'Do you know, Lapierre, you've just given me the subject of a novel, the counterpart of my *Bovary*, a *Bovary* of high society. What an attractive figure!' He copied down the story at once, and began to make notes on it. But the novel was never written, and the notes have never been found.

All these unwritten books tantalise. Yet they can, to an extent, be filled out, ordered, reimagined. They can be studied in academies. A pier is a disappointed bridge; yet stare at it for long enough and you can dream it to the other side of the Channel. The same is true with these stubs of books.

But what of the unled lives? These, perhaps, are more truly tantalising; these are the real apocrypha. *Thermopylae* instead of *Bouvard et Pécuchet*? Well, it's still a book. But if Gustave himself had changed course? It's easy, after all, not to be a writer. Most people aren't writers, and very little harm comes to them. A phrenologist – that careers master of the nineteenth century – once examined Flaubert and told him he was cut out to be a tamer of wild beasts. Not so inaccurate either. That quote again: 'I attract mad people and animals'.

It is not just the life that we know. It is not just the life that has been successfully hidden. It is not just the lies about the life, some of which cannot now be disbelieved. It is also the life that was not led.

'Am I to be a king, or just a pig?' Gustave writes in his *Intimate Notebook*. At nineteen, it always looks as simple as this. There is the life, and then there is the not-life; the life of ambition served, or the life of porcine failure. Others try and tell you about your future, but you never really believe them. 'Many things', Gustave writes at this time, 'have been predicted to me: 1) that I'll learn to dance; 2) that I'll marry. We'll see – I don't believe it.'

He never married, and he never learned to dance. He was so resistant to dancing that most of the principal male characters in his novels take sympathetic action and refuse to dance as well.

What did he learn instead? Instead he learned that life is not a choice between murdering your way to the throne or slopping back in a sty; that there are swinish kings and regal hogs; that the king may envy the pig; and that the possibilities of the not-life will always change tormentingly to fit the particular embarrassments of the lived life.

At seventeen, he announces that he wants to spend his whole life in a ruined castle by the sea.

At eighteen, he decides that some freakish wind must have mistakenly transplanted him to France: he was born, he declares, to be Emperor of Cochin-China, to smoke 36-fathom pipes, to have 6,000 wives and 1,400 catamites; but instead, displaced by this meteorological hazard, he is left with immense, insatiable desires, fierce boredom, and an attack of the yawns.

At nineteen, he thinks that after he's finished his legal studies he'll go off and become a Turk in Turkey, or a muleteer in Spain, or a cameleer in Egypt.

At twenty, he still wants to become a muleteer, though by now the Spanish location has been narrowed to that of Andalusia. Other career possibilities include the life of a lazzarone in Naples; though he'd settle for being the driver of the coach which plies between Nîmes and Marseilles. Yet is any of this rare enough? The ease with which even the bourgeois travel nowadays comes as an agony to one who has 'the Bosphorus in the soul'.

At twenty-four, with his father and sister newly dead, he plans what to do with his life should his mother die as well: he would sell up everything and live in Rome, Syracuse or Naples.

Still twenty-four, and presenting himself to Louise Colet as a fellow of infinite whim, he claims that he has thought long and *very seriously* about the idea of becoming a bandit in Smyrna. But at the very least 'some day I shall go and live far away from here and never be heard of again'. Perhaps Louise is little amused by Ottoman banditry; for now a more domestic fantasy appears. If only he were free, he would leave Croisset and come to live with her in Paris. He imagines their life together, their marriage, a sweet existence of mutual love and mutual companionship. He imagines their having a child together; he imagines Louise's death and his own subsequent tenderness in caring for the motherless infant (we do not, alas, have Louise's response to this particular flight). The exotic appeal of the domestic does not, however, last. Within a month the tense of the verb curdles: 'It seems to me that if I had been your husband, we would have been happy together. After we'd been happy, then we would have hated one another. This is normal.' Louise is expected to be grateful that Gustave's far-sightedness has spared her such an unsatisfactory life.

So instead, and still twenty-four, Gustave sits over a map with Du Camp and plans a monster journey to Asia. It would last six years and would cost, at their own rough estimate, three million six hundred thousand and a few odd francs.

At twenty-five he wants to be a Brahmin: the mystic dance, the long hair, the face dripping with holy butter. He officially renounces wanting to be a Camaldolese, a brigand or a Turk. 'Now it's a Brahmin, or nothing at all — which would be simpler.' Go on, be nothing at all, life urges. Being a pig is simple.

At twenty-nine, inspired by Humboldt, he wants to go off and live in South America, among the savannahs, and never be heard of again.

At thirty he muses — as he did throughout his life — on his own previous incarnations, on his apocryphal or metempsychotic lives in the more interesting times of Louis XIV, Nero and Pericles. Of one preincarnation he is certain: he was, at some point during the Roman Empire, the director of a troupe of travelling comedians, the sort of plausible rogue who bought women in Sicily and turned them into actresses, a rowdy mixture of teacher, pimp and artist. (Reading Plautus has reminded Gustave of this previous life: it gives him *le frisson historique*.) Here we should also note Gustave's apocryphal ancestry: he liked to claim that he had Red Indian blood in his veins. This seems to have been not quite the case; though one of his ancestors did emigrate to Canada in the seventeenth century and become a beaver-trapper.

Still thirty, he projects a seemingly more probable life, but one which proves equally to be a not-life. He and Bouilhet play at imagining themselves old men, patients in some hospice for incurables: ancients who sweep the streets and babble to one another of that happy time when they were both thirty and walked all the way to La Roche-Guyon. The mocked senility was never attained: Bouilhet died at forty-eight, Flaubert at fifty-eight.

At thirty-one, he remarks to Louise — a parenthesis to a hypothesis

— that if he *had* ever had a son, he would have taken great pleasure in procuring women for him.

Also at thirty-one, he reports a brief, untypical lapse to Louise: the desire to chuck in literature. He will come and live with her, inside her, his head between her breasts; he is fed up, he says, with masturbating that head of his to make the phrases spurt. But this fantasy is also a chilling tease: it's recounted in the past tense, as something which Gustave, in a moment of weakness, fleetingly imagined himself doing. He would always rather have his head between his own hands than between Louise's breasts.

At thirty-two, he confesses to Louise the manner in which he has spent many hours of his life: imagining what he would do if he had an income of a million francs a year. In such dreams servants would ease him into shoes studded with diamonds; he would cock an ear to the whinny of his coach-horses, whose splendour would make England die of jealousy; he would give oyster banquets, and have his dining-room surrounded by espaliers of flowering jasmine, out of which bright finches would swoop. But this, at a million a year, was a cheap dream. Du Camp reports Gustave's plans for 'A Winter in Paris' — an extravaganza incorporating the luxury of the Roman Empire, the refinement of the Renaissance, and the faerie of the Thousand and One Nights. The Winter had been seriously costed, and it came out at twelve thousand million francs 'at the most'. Du Camp also adds, more generally, that 'when these dreams took possession of him, he became almost rigid, and reminded one of an opium-eater in a state of trance. He seemed to have his head in the clouds, to be living in a dream of gold. This habit was one reason why he found steady work difficult.'

At thirty-five, he reveals 'my private dream': to buy a little *palazzo* on the Grand Canal. A few months later, a kiosk on the Bosphorus is added to the real estate in his head. A few months more, and he is ready to leave for the East, to stay there, to die there. The painter Camille Rogier, who lives in Beirut, has invited him. He could go; just like that. He could; he doesn't.

At thirty-five, however, the apocryphal life, the not-life, begins to die away. The reason is clear: the real life has really begun. Gustave was thirty-five when *Madame Bovary* came out in book form. The fantasies are no longer needed; or rather, different, particular, practical fantasies are now required. For the world, he will play the Hermit of Croisset; for his friends in Paris, he will play the Idiot of the Salons; for George Sand he will play the Reverend Father Cruchard, a fashionable Jesuit who enjoys hearing the confessions of society women; for his intimate circle he will play Saint Polycarpe, that obscure Bishop of Smyrna, martyred in the nick of time at the age of ninety-five, who pre-echoed Flaubert by stopping up his ears and crying out, 'Oh Lord! Into what an age you have caused me to be born!' But these identities are no longer lurid alibis towards which he might credibly escape; they are playthings, alternative lives issued under licence by the celebrated author. He does not run off to become a bandit in Smyrna; instead, he summons the useful Bishop of Smyrna to live within his skin. He has proved not a tamer of wild beasts, but a tamer of wild lives. Pacification of the apocryphal is complete: writing can begin.

IO

The Case Against

What makes us want to know the worst? Is it that we tire of preferring to know the best? Does curiosity always hurdle self-interest? Or is it, more simply, that wanting to know the worst is love's favourite perversion?

For some, this curiosity operates as baleful fantasy. I had a patient once, a respectable nine-to-fiver otherwise untouched by imagination, who confessed that while making love to his wife he liked to picture her spread blissfully beneath mountainous hidalgos, sleek lascars, rummaging dwarfs. Shock me, the fantasy urges, appal me. For others, the search is real. I have known couples take pride in one another's tawdry behaviour: each pursuing the other's folly, the other's vanity, the other's weakness. What were they really after? Something, evidently, which lay beyond what they appeared to seek. Perhaps some final confirmation that mankind itself was ineradicably corrupt, that life was indeed just a gaudy nightmare in the head of an imbecile?

I loved Ellen, and I wanted to know the worst. I never provoked her; I was cautious and defensive, as is my habit; I didn't even ask questions; but I wanted to know the worst. Ellen never returned this caress. She was fond of me — she would automatically agree, as if the matter weren't worth discussing, that she loved me — but she unquestioningly believed the best about me. That's the difference.

She didn't ever search for that sliding panel which opens the secret chamber of the heart, the chamber where memory and corpses are kept. Sometimes you find the panel, but it doesn't open; sometimes it opens, and your gaze meets nothing but a mouse skeleton. But at least you've looked. That's the real distinction between people: not between those who have secrets and those who don't, but between those who want to know everything and those who don't. This search is a sign of love, I maintain.

It's similar with books. Not quite the same, of course (it never is); but similar. If you quite enjoy a writer's work, if you turn the page approvingly yet don't mind being interrupted, then you tend to like that author unthinkingly. Good chap, you assume. Sound fellow. They say he strangled an entire pack of Wolf Cubs and fed their bodies to a school of carp? Oh no, I'm sure he didn't: sound fellow, good chap. But if you love a writer, if you depend upon the drip-feed of his intelligence, if you want to pursue him and find him — despite edicts to the contrary — then it's impossible to know too much. You seek the vice as well. A pack of Wolf Cubs, eh? Was that twenty-seven or twenty-eight? And did he have their little scarves sewn up into a patchwork quilt? And is it true that as he ascended the scaffold he quoted from the Book of Jonah? And that he bequeathed his carp pond to the local Boy Scouts?

But here's the difference. With a lover, a wife, when you find the worst — be it infidelity or lack of love, madness or the suicidal spark — you are almost relieved. Life is as I thought it was; shall we now celebrate this disappointment? With a writer you love, the instinct is to defend. This is what I meant earlier: perhaps love for a writer is the purest, the steadiest form of love. And so your defence comes the more easily. The fact of the matter is, carp are an endangered species, and everyone knows that the only diet they will accept if the winter has been especially harsh and the spring turns wet before St Oursin's Day is that of young minced Wolf Cub. Of course he knew he would hang for the offence, but he also knew that humanity is not an endangered species, and reckoned therefore that twenty-seven (did you say twenty-eight?) Wolf Cubs plus one middle-ranking author (he was always ridiculously modest about his talents) were a trivial price to pay for the survival of an entire breed of fish. Take the long view: did we need so many Wolf Cubs? They would only have grown up and become Boy Scouts. And if you're still mired in sentimentality, look at it this way: the admission fees so far received from visitors to the carp pond have already enabled the Boy Scouts to build and maintain several church halls in the area.

So go on. Read the charge-sheet. I had expected it at some point. But don't forget this: Gustave has been in the dock before. How many offences are there this time?

1 *That he hated humanity.*

Yes, yes, of course. You always say that. I'll give you two sorts of answer. First, let's start with basics. He loved his mother: doesn't that warm your silly, sentimental, twentieth-century heart? He loved his father. He loved his sister. He loved his niece. He loved his friends. He admired certain individuals. But his affections were always specific; they were not given away to all-comers. This seems enough to me. You want him to do more? You want him to 'love humanity', to goose the human race? But that means nothing. Loving humanity means as much and as little as loving raindrops, or loving the Milky Way. You say that you love humanity? Are you sure you aren't treating yourself to easy self-congratulation, seeking approval, making certain you're on the right side?

Secondly, even if he did hate humanity — or was profoundly unimpressed by it, as I would prefer to say — was he wrong? You, clearly, are quite impressed by humanity: it's all clever irrigation schemes, missionary work and micro-electronics to you. Forgive him for seeing it differently. It's clear we're going to have to discuss this at some length. But let me first, briefly, quote to you one of your wise men of the twentieth century: Freud. Not, you will agree, someone with an axe to grind? You want his summing-up on the human race, ten years before his death? 'In the depths of my heart I can't help being convinced that my dear fellow-men, with a few exceptions, are worthless.' This from the man that most people, for most of this century, believed most thoroughly understood the human heart. It is a little embarrassing, is it not?

But come, it's time for you to be rather more specific.

2 *That he hated democracy.*

La democrasserie, as he called it in a letter to Taine. Which do you prefer — democrappery or democrassness? Democrappiness, perhaps? He was, it is true, very unimpressed by it. From which you should not conclude that he favoured tyranny, or absolute monarchy, or bourgeois monarchy, or bureaucratised totalitarianism, or anarchy, or whatever. His preferred model of government was a Chinese one — that of the Mandarinate; though he readily admitted that its chances of introduction into France were extremely small. The Mandarinate seems a step back to you? But you forgive Voltaire his enthusiasm for enlightened monarchy: why not forgive Flaubert, a century later, his enthusiasm for enlightened oligarchy? He did not, at least, entertain the childish fantasy of some literati: that writers are better fitted to run the world than anybody else.

The main point is this: Flaubert thought democracy merely a stage in the history of government, and he thought it a typical vanity on our part to assume that it represented the finest, proudest way for men to rule one another. He believed in — or rather, he did not fail to notice — the perpetual evolution of humanity, and therefore the evolution of its social forms: 'Democracy isn't mankind's last word, any more than slavery was, or feudalism was, or monarchy was.' The best form of government, he maintained, is one that is dying, because this means it's giving way to something else.

3 *That he didn't believe in progress.*

I cite the twentieth century in his defence.

4 *That he wasn't interested enough in politics.*

Interested 'enough'? You admit, at least, that he was interested. You are suggesting, tactfully, that he didn't like what he saw (correct), and that if he had seen more, he would perhaps have come round to your way of thinking in these matters (incorrect). I should like to make two points, the first of which I shall put into italics, since this seems to be your favourite mode of utterance. *Literature includes politics, and not vice versa.* This isn't a fashionable view, neither with writers nor politicians, but you will forgive me. Novelists who think their writing an instrument of politics seem to me to degrade writing and foolishly exalt politics. No, I'm not saying they should be forbidden from having political opinions or from making political statements. It's just that they should call that part of their work journalism. The writer who imagines that the novel is the most effective way of taking part in politics is usually a bad novelist, a bad journalist, and a bad politician.

Du Camp followed politics carefully, Flaubert sporadically. Which do you prefer? The former. And which of them was the greater writer? The latter. And what were their politics? Du Camp became a lethargic meliorist; Flaubert remained 'an enraged liberal'. Does that surprise you? But even if Flaubert had described himself as a lethargic meliorist, I should make the same point: what a curious vanity it is of the present to expect the past to suck up to it. The present looks back at some great figure of an earlier century and wonders, Was he on our side? Was he a goodie? What a lack of self-confidence this implies: the present wants both to patronise the past by adjudicating on its political acceptability, and also to be flattered by it, to be patted on the back and told to keep up the good work. If this is what you understand by Monsieur Flaubert not being 'interested enough' in politics, then I'm afraid my client must plead guilty.

5 *That he was against the Commune.*

Well, what I've said above is part of the answer. But there is also this consideration, this incredible weakness of character on my client's part: he was on the whole against people killing one another. Call it squeamishness, but he did disapprove. He never killed anyone himself, I have to admit; in fact, he never even tried. He promises to do better in future.

6 *That he was unpatriotic.*

Permit me a short laugh. Ah. That's better. I thought patriotism was a bad thing nowadays. I thought we would all rather betray our country than our friends. Is that not so? Have things turned upside down yet again? What am I expected to say? On September 22nd, 1870, Flaubert bought himself a revolver; at Croisset, he drilled his ragged collection of men in expectation of a Prussian advance; he took them out on night patrols; he told them to shoot him if he tried to run away. By the time the Prussians came, there was not much he could sensibly do except look after his aged mother. He could perhaps have submitted himself to some army medical board, but whether they would have enthused over the application of a 48-year-old epileptic syphilitic with no military experience except that acquired while shooting wild-life in the desert —

7 *That he shot wild-life in the desert.*

Oh, for Christ's sake. We plead *noli contendere*. And besides I haven't finished with the question of patriotism. May I instruct you briefly on the nature of the novelist? What is the easiest, the most comfortable thing for a writer to do? To congratulate the society in which he lives: to admire its biceps, applaud its progress, tease it endearingly about its follies. 'I am as much a Chinaman as a Frenchman,' Flaubert declared. Not, that is, *more* of a Chinaman: had he been born in Peking, no doubt he would have disappointed patriots there too. The greatest patriotism is to tell your country when it is behaving dishonourably, foolishly, viciously. The writer must be universal in sympathy and an outcast by nature: only then can he see clearly. Flaubert always sides with minorities, with 'the Bedouin, the Heretic, the philosopher, the hermit, the Poet'. In 1867 forty-three gypsies pitched camp in the Cours la Reine and aroused much hatred among the Rouennais. Flaubert delighted in their presence and gave them money. No doubt you wish to pat him on the head for this. If he'd known he was gaining the approval of the future, he'd probably have kept the money to himself.

8 *That he didn't involve himself in life.*

'You can depict wine, love, women and glory on the condition that you're not a drunkard, a lover, a husband or a private in the ranks. If you participate in life, you don't see it clearly: you suffer from it too much or enjoy it too much.' This isn't a reply of guilty, it's a complaint that the charge is wrongly phrased. What do you mean by life? Politics? We've dealt with that. The emotional life? Through his family, friends and mistresses, Gustave knew all the stations of the cross. Marriage, you mean perhaps? A curious complaint, though not a new one. Does marriage produce better novels than bachelorhood? Are the philoprogenitive better writers than the childless? I should like to see your statistics.

The best life for a writer is the life which helps him write the best books he can. Are we confident that our judgment in the matter is better than his? Flaubert was more 'involved', to use your term, than many: Henry James by comparison was a nun. Flaubert may have tried to live in an ivory tower —

8 a) *That he tried to live in an ivory tower.*

but he failed. 'I have always tried to live in an ivory tower, but a tide of shit is beating at its walls, threatening to undermine it.'

Three points need to be made. One is that the writer chooses — as far as he can — the extent of what you call his involvement in life: despite his reputation, Flaubert occupied a half-and-half position. 'It isn't the drunkard who writes the drinking song': he knew that. On the other hand, it isn't the teetotaller either. He put it best, perhaps, when he said that the writer must wade into life as into the sea, but only up to the navel.

Secondly, when readers complain about the lives of writers — why didn't he do this; why didn't he protest to the newspapers about that; why wasn't he more involved in life? — aren't they really asking a simpler, and vainer, question: why isn't he more like us? But if a writer were more like a reader, he'd be a reader, not a writer: it's as uncomplicated as that.

Thirdly, what is the thrust of the complaint as far as the books are concerned? Presumably the regret that Flaubert wasn't more involved in life isn't just a philanthropic wish for him: if only old Gustave had had a wife and kiddies, he wouldn't have been so glum about the whole shooting-match? If only he'd got caught up in politics, or good works, or become a governor of his old school, he'd have been taken out of himself more? Presumably you think there are faults in the books which could have been remedied by a change in the writer's life. If so, I think it is up to you to state them. For myself, I cannot think that, for instance, the portrait of provincial manners in *Madame Bovary* is lacking in some particular aspect which would have been remedied had its author clinked tankards of cider every evening with some gouty Norman *bergère*.

9 *That he was a pessimist.*

Ah. I begin to see what you mean. You wish his books were a bit more cheerful, a bit more . . . how would you put it, life-enhancing? What a curious idea of literature you do have. Is your PhD from Bucharest? I didn't know one had to defend authors for being pessimists. This is a new one. I decline to do so. Flaubert said: 'You don't make art out of good intentions.' He also said: 'The public wants works which flatter its illusions.'

10 *That he teaches no positive virtues*.

Now you are coming out into the open. So this is how we are to judge our writers — on their 'positive virtues'? Well, I suppose I must play your game briefly: it's what you have to do in the courts. Take all the obscenity trials from *Madame Bovary* to *Lady Chatterley's Lover*: there's always some element of games-playing, of compliance, in the defence. Others might call it tactical hypocrisy. (Is this book sexy? No, M'Lud, we hold that it would have an emetic, not a mimetic, effect on any reader. Does this book encourage adultery? No, M'Lud, look how the miserable sinner who gives herself time and time again to riotous pleasure is punished in the end. Does this book attack marriage? No, M'Lud, it portrays a vile and hopeless marriage so that others may learn that only by following Christian instructions will their own marriages be happy. Is this book blasphemous? No, M'Lud, the novelist's thought is chaste.) As a forensic argument, of course, it has been successful; but I sometimes feel a residual bitterness that one of these defence counsel, when speaking for a true work of literature, did not build his act on simple defiance. (Is this book sexy? M'Lud, we bloody well hope so. Does it encourage adultery and attack marriage? Spot on, M'Lud, that's *exactly* what my client is trying to do. Is this book blasphemous? For Christ's sake, M'Lud, the matter's as clear as the loincloth on the Crucifixion. Put it this way, M'Lud: my client thinks that most of the values of the society in which he lives stink, and he hopes with this book to promote fornication, masturbation, adultery, the stoning of priests and, since we've temporarily got your attention, M'Lud, the suspension of corrupt judges by their earlobes. The defence rests its case.)

So, briefly: Flaubert teaches you to gaze upon the truth and not blink from its consequences; he teaches you, with Montaigne, to sleep on the pillow of doubt; he teaches you to dissect out the constituent parts of reality, and to observe that Nature is always a mixture of genres; he teaches you the most exact use of language; he teaches you not to approach a book in search of moral or social pills — literature is not a pharmacopoeia; he teaches the pre-eminence of Truth, Beauty, Feeling and Style. And if you study his private life, he teaches courage, stoicism, friendship; the importance of intelligence, scepticism and wit; the folly of cheap patriotism; the virtue of being able to remain by yourself in your own room; the hatred of hypocrisy; distrust of the doctrinaire; the need for plain speaking. Is that the way you like writers to be described (I do not care for it much myself)? Is it enough? It's all I'm giving you for the moment: I seem to be embarrassing my client.

11 *That he was a Sadist.*

Rubbish. My client was a soft touch. Cite me a single sadistic, or even unkind, thing he did in his whole life. I'll tell you the unkindest thing I know about him: he was caught being beastly to a woman at a party for no obvious reason. When asked why, he replied, 'Because she might want to come into my study.' That's the worst thing I know about my client. Unless you count the occasion in Egypt when he tried to go to bed with a prostitute while suffering from the pox. That was a little deceitful, I admit. But he didn't succeed: the girl, following the normal precautions of her profession, asked to examine him and, when he refused, sent him packing.

He read Sade, of course. What educated French writer doesn't? I gather he is currently popular among Parisian intellectuals. My client told the Goncourt brothers that Sade was 'entertaining nonsense'. He kept a few gruesome mementoes around him, it is true; he enjoyed recounting horrors; there are lurid passages in his early work. But you say he had a 'Sadeian imagination'? I am puzzled. You specify: *Salammbô* contains scenes of shocking violence. I reply: do you think they didn't happen? Do you think the Ancient World was all rose petals, lute music, and plump vats of honey sealed with bear fat?

11 a) *That there are a lot of animals slaughtered in his books.*

He isn't Walt Disney, no. He was interested in cruelty, I agree. He was interested in everything. As well as Sade, there was Nero. But listen to what he says about them: 'These monsters explain history for me.' He is, I must add, all of seventeen at the time. And let me give you another quote: 'I love the vanquished, but I also love the victors.' He strives, as I've said, to be as much a Chinaman as a Frenchman. There is an earthquake in Leghorn: Flaubert doesn't cry out in sympathy. He feels as much sympathy for these victims as he does for slaves who died centuries earlier turning some tyrant's grindstone. You are shocked? It's called having a historical imagination. It's called being a citizen, not just of the world, but of all time. It's what Flaubert described as being 'brother in God to everything that lives, from the giraffe and the crocodile to man.' It's called being a writer.

12 *That he was beastly to women.*

Women loved him. He enjoyed their company; they enjoyed his; he was gallant, flirtatious; he went to bed with them. He just didn't want to marry them. Is that a sin? Perhaps some of his sexual attitudes were pungently those of his time and his class; but who then in the nineteenth century shall escape whipping? He stood, at least, for honesty in sexual dealings: hence his preference for the prostitute over the *grisette*. Such honesty brought him more trouble than hypocrisy would have done — with Louise Colet, for instance. When he told her the truth it sounded like cruelty. But she was a pest, wasn't she? (Let me answer my own question. I think she was a pest; she sounds like a pest; though admittedly we hear only Gustave's side of the story. Perhaps someone should write her account: yes, why not reconstruct Louise Colet's Version? I might do that. Yes, I will.)

If I may say so, a lot of your charges could probably be reclassified under a single heading: *That he wouldn't have liked us if he'd known us.* To which he might be inclined to plead guilty; if only to see the expression on our face.

13 *That he believed in Beauty.*

I think I've got something lodged in my ear. Probably a bit of wax. Just give me a moment to grip my nose and blow out through my eardrums.

14 *That he was obsessed with style.*

You are babbling. Do you still think the novel divides, like Gaul, into three parts — the Idea, the Form and the Style? If so, you are taking your own first tremulous steps into fiction. You want some maxims for writing? Very well. Form isn't an overcoat flung over the flesh of thought (that old comparison, old in Flaubert's day); it's the flesh of thought itself. You can no more imagine an Idea without a Form than a Form without an Idea. Everything in art depends on execution: the story of a louse can be as beautiful as the story of Alexander. You must write according to your feelings, be sure those feelings are true, and let everything else go hang. When a line is good, it ceases to belong to any school. A line of prose must be as immutable as a line of poetry. If you happen to write well, you are accused of lacking ideas.

All these maxims are by Flaubert, except for the one by Bouilhet.

15 *That he didn't believe Art had a social purpose.*

No, he didn't. This is wearying. 'You provide desolation,' wrote George Sand, 'and I provide consolation.' To which Flaubert replied, 'I cannot change my eyes.' The work of art is a pyramid which stands in the desert, uselessly: jackals piss at the base of it, and bourgeois clamber to the top of it; continue this comparison. Do you want art to be a healer? Send for the AMBULANCE GEORGE SAND. Do you want art to tell the truth? Send for the AMBULANCE FLAUBERT: though don't be surprised, when it arrives, if it runs over your leg. Listen to Auden: 'Poetry makes nothing happen.' Do not imagine that Art is something which is designed to give gentle uplift and self-confidence. Art is not a *brassière*. At least, not in the English sense. But do not forget that *brassière* is the French for life-jacket.

II

Louise Colet's Version

Now hear my story. I insist. Look, take my arm, like that, and let's just walk. I have tales to tell; you will like them. We'll follow the quai, and cross that bridge — no, the second one — and perhaps we could take a cognac somewhere, and wait until the gas-lamps dim, and then walk back. Come, you're surely not frightened of me? So why that look? You think I am a dangerous woman? Well, that's a form of flattery — I accept the compliment. Or perhaps . . . perhaps it's what I might have to *say* that you're frightened of? Aha . . . well, it's too late now. You have taken my arm; you cannot drop it. After all, I am older than you. It is your job to protect me.

I have no interest in slander. Slip your fingers down my forearm, if you want to; yes, there, now feel the pulse. I am not vengeful tonight. Some friends say, Louise, you must answer fire with fire, lie with lie. But I do not wish to. Of course I have lied in my time; I have — what is that word your sex favours? — I have schemed. But women scheme when they are weak, they lie out of fear. Men scheme when they are strong, they lie out of arrogance. You don't agree? I only speak from observation; yours may be different, I grant. But you see how calm I am? I am calm because I feel strong. And — what's that? Perhaps, if I am strong, then I am scheming like a man? Come, let's not be complicated.

I did not need Gustave to come into my life. Look at the facts. I was thirty-five, I was beautiful, I was . . . renowned. I had conquered first Aix, then Paris. I had won the Académie's poetry prize twice. I had translated Shakespeare. Victor Hugo called me *sister*; Béranger called me *Muse*. As for my private life: my husband was respected in his profession; my . . . protector was the most brilliant philosopher of his age. You haven't read Victor Cousin? Then you should. A fascinating mind. The only man who truly understood Plato. A friend of your philosopher Mr Mill. And then, there was — or there was soon to be — Musset, Vigny, Champfleury. I do not boast of my conquests; I do not need to. But you see my point. I was the candle; he was the moth. The mistress of Socrates deigned to cast her smile on this unknown poet. *I* was *his* catch; he wasn't mine.

We met at Pradier's. I could see the banality of that; though of course he couldn't. The sculptor's studio, the free talk, the unclothed model, the mixture of demi-monde and three-quarter-monde. To me it was all familiar (why, only a few years before I'd danced there with a stiff-backed medical student by the name of Achille Flaubert). And, of course, I wasn't present as a spectator; I was there to sit for Pradier. Whereas Gustave? I do not want to be harsh, but when I first set eyes on him I knew the type at once: the big, gangling provincial, so eager and relieved to find himself at last in artistic circles. I know how they talk, out in the provinces, with that mixture of fake self-confidence and real fear: 'Go to Pradier's, my boy, you'll always find some little actress there to be your mistress, and grateful she'll be too.' And the boy in Toulouse or Poitiers or Bordeaux or Rouen, still secretly anxious about the long journey to the capital, feels his head filling up with snobbery and lust. I *understood*, you see, because I had been a provincial myself. I had made the journey from Aix a dozen years earlier. I had come a long way; and I could recognise the signs of travel in others.

Gustave was twenty-four. To my mind, age does not matter; love is what matters. I did not need to have Gustave in my life. If I had been looking for a lover — I admit my husband's fortunes were not at their brightest, and my friendship with the Philosopher was a little turbulent at that time — then I should not have chosen Gustave. But I have no stomach for fat bankers. And besides, you do not look, you do not choose, do you? You are chosen; you are elected into love by a secret ballot against which there is no appeal.

I do not blush at the difference between our ages? Why should I? You men are so conformist in love, so provincial in imagination; that is why we have to flatter you, to prop you up with little lies. So: I was thirty-five, Gustave was twenty-four. I state it and pass on. Perhaps you do not want to pass on; in which case I shall answer your unspoken question. If you wish to examine the mental condition of the couple entering into such a liaison, then you do not need to look at mine. Examine Gustave's. Why? I will give you a pair of dates. I was born in 1810, in September, the 15th day of the month. You remember Gustave's Madame Schlesinger, the woman who first cicatrised his adolescent heart, the woman with whom everything was doomed and hopeless, the woman of whom he used to boast furtively, the woman for whose sake he had bricked up his heart (and you accuse *our* sex of vain romance?). Well, this Mme Schlesinger, I happen to know, was also born in 1810, and also in September. Eight days after me, to be precise, on the 23rd. You see?

You look at me in a way that is familiar. I surmise that you want me to tell you how Gustave was as a lover. Men, I know, talk of such things with eagerness, with a little contempt; it is as if they were describing the last meal they had, course by course. So much detachment. Women are not like that; or at least, the details, the weaknesses they dwell on in narration are only rarely the physical ones that men delight in. We look for signs that speak to us of character — good or bad. Men look only for signs which flatter them. They are so vain in bed, much more vain than women. Outside, the sexes are more evenly matched, I admit.

I will reply a little more freely, because you are who you are; and because it is Gustave of whom I speak. He always used to lecture people, tell them about the honesty of the artist, the necessity not to speak like a bourgeois. Well, if I lift the sheets a little, he has only himself to blame.

He was eager, my Gustave. It was — God knows — never easy to persuade him to meet me; but once he was there ... Whatever the battles that occurred between us, none of them was fought in the province of the night. There, we embraced by lightning; there, violent wonder lay entwined with soft playfulness. He carried a bottle of water from the River Mississippi with which, he said, he planned to baptise my breast as a sign of love. He was a strong young man, and I delighted in that strength: he once signed a letter to me 'Your wild boy of Aveyron'.

He had, of course, the eternal delusion of strong young men, that women gauge passion by counting the number of times that the assault is renewed in the course of a single night. Well, to some extent we do: who would deny that? It is flattering, is it not? But it is not what counts finally. And after a while, there seems something almost military about it. Gustave had a way of talking about the women he had enjoyed. He would recall some prostitute he had frequented in the rue de la Cigogne: 'I fired five shots into her,' he would boast to me. It was his habitual turn of phrase. I found it coarse, but I did not mind: we were artists together, you see. However, I noted the metaphor. The more shots you fire into somebody, the more likely they are to be dead at the end of it. Is that what men want? Do they need a corpse as proof of their virility? I suspect they do, and women, with the logic of flattery, remember to exclaim at the transporting moment, 'Oh, I die! I die!' or some such phrase. After a bout of love, I often find that my brain is at its sharpest; I see things clearly; I feel poetry coming to me. But I know better than to interrupt the hero with my babblings; instead I ape the satisfied cadaver.

In the province of the night there was harmony between us. Gustave was not shy. Nor was he narrow in his tastes. I was — why should I be modest — undoubtedly the most beautiful, the most renowned, the most desirable woman with whom he ever slept (if I had any rival, it was only a strange beast I shall tell you of later). He was, naturally, sometimes nervous in the face of my beauty; and at other times needlessly pleased with himself. I understood. Before me there had been prostitutes, of course, *grisettes*, and friends. Ernest, Alfred, Louis, Max: the band of students, that was how I thought of them. Sodality confirmed by sodomy. No, perhaps that's unfair; I do not know precisely who, precisely when, precisely what;

though I do know that Gustave was never tired of *double ententes* about *la pipe*. I also know he was never tired of gazing at me as I lay on my front.

I was different, you see. Prostitutes were uncomplicated; *grisettes* could be paid off too; men were different — friendship, however deep, had its known limits. But love? And losing yourself? And some partnership, some equality? He didn't dare risk it. I was the only woman to whom he was sufficiently drawn; and he chose, out of fear, to humiliate me. I think we should feel sorry for Gustave.

He used to send me flowers. Special flowers; the convention of an unconventional lover. He sent me a rose once. He gathered it one Sunday morning at Croisset, from a hedge in his garden. 'I kiss it,' he wrote. 'Put it quickly to your mouth, and then — you know where . . . Adieu! A thousand kisses. I am yours from night to day, from day to night.' Who could resist such sentiments? I kissed the rose, and that night, in bed, I placed it where he desired me to. In the morning, when I awoke, the rose had by the motions of the night been reduced to its fragrant parts. The sheets smelt of Croisset — that place which I did not yet know would be forbidden to me; there was a petal between two of my toes, and a thin scratch down the inside of my right thigh. Gustave, eager and clumsy as he was, had forgotten to smooth the stem of the rose.

The next flower was not such a happy one. Gustave went off on his tour of Brittany. Was I wrong to make a fuss? Three months! We had known one another less than a year, all Paris knew of our passion, and he chose three months in the company of Du Camp! We could have been like George Sand and Chopin; greater than them! And Gustave insists on disappearing for three months with that ambitious catamite of his. Was I wrong to make a fuss? Was it not a direct insult, an attempt to humiliate me? And yet *he* said, when I expressed my feelings to him in public (I am not ashamed of love — why should I be? I would declare myself in the waiting-room of a railway station if it were necessary), *he* said that *I* was humiliating *him*. Imagine! He cast me off. *Ultima*, I wrote on the last letter he sent me before his departure.

It wasn't, of course, his last letter. No sooner was he striding across that tedious countryside, pretending to be interested in disused châteaux and drab churches (three months!) then he began to miss me. The letters started to arrive, the apologies, the confessions, the pleas that I should reply to him. He was always like that. When he was at Croisset, he dreamed of the hot sand and the shimmering Nile; when he was on the Nile, he dreamed of damp fogs and shimmering Croisset. He didn't really like travel, of course. He liked the idea of travel, and the memory of travel, but not travel itself. For once I agree with Du Camp, who used to say that Gustave's preferred form of travel was to lie on a divan and have the scenery carried past him. As for that famous Oriental trip of theirs, Du Camp (yes, the odious Du Camp, the unreliable Du Camp) maintained that Gustave spent most of the journey in a state of torpor.

But anyway: while he was tramping through that dull and backward province with his malign companion, Gustave sent me another flower, plucked from beside the tomb of Châteaubriand. He wrote of the calm sea at St Malo, the pink sky, the sweet air. It makes a fine scene, does it not? The romantic grave on that rocky promontory; the great man lying there, his head pointing out to sea, listening for all eternity to the comings and goings of the tide; the young writer, with stirrings of genius inside him, kneels by the tomb, watches the pink drain slowly from the evening sky, reflects — in the way young men are wont to do — on eternity, the fugitive nature of life and the consolations of greatness, then gathers a flower which has rooted itself in Châteaubriand's dust, and sends it to his beautiful mistress in Paris . . . Could I be unmoved by such a gesture? Of course not. But I could not help observing that a flower plucked from a grave brings with it certain reverberations when sent to one who has written *Ultima* on a letter received not long before. And I also could not help observing that Gustave's letter was posted from Pontorson, which is forty kilometres from St Malo. Did Gustave pick the flower for himself and then, after forty kilometres, grow weary of it? Or perhaps — such a suggestion arises in me only because I have lain next to the contagious soul of Gustave himself — did he gather it elsewhere? Did he think of the gesture a little too late? Who can resist *l'esprit de l'escalier*, even in love?

My flower — the one that I remember best out of many — was gathered where I said it had been. In Windsor Park. It was after my tragic visit to Croisset and the humiliation of not being received, after the brutality, the pain and the horror of it all. You have heard different versions, no doubt? The truth is simple.

I had to see him. We had to talk. You do not dismiss love in the way you dismiss your hairdresser. He would not come to me in Paris; so I went to him. I took the train (beyond Mantes, this time) to Rouen. I was rowed downstream to Croisset; in my soul, hope struggled with fear, while the ancient oarsman struggled with the current. We came in sight of a charming, low white house in the English style; a laughing house, as it seemed to me. I disembarked; I pushed the iron grille; I was allowed no further. Gustave refused me entrance. Some barnyard crone turned me away. He would not see me there; he condescended to see me at my hotel. My Charon rowed me back. Gustave travelled separately by steamer. He overtook us on the river and arrived ahead of me. It was farce, it was tragedy. We went to my hotel. I talked, but he could not hear. I spoke of possible happiness. The secret of happiness, he told me, is to be happy already. He did not understand my anguish. He embraced me with a self-restraint that was humiliating. He told me to marry Victor Cousin.

I fled to England. I could not bear tŏ be in France a moment longer: my friends confirmed my impulse. I went to London. I was received there with kindness. I was introduced to many distinguished spirits. I met Mazzini; I met the Countess Guiccioli. My meeting with the Countess was an uplifting occasion — we became firm friends at once — but also, privately, a saddening one. George Sand and Chopin, the Countess Guiccioli and Byron . . . would they ever say Louise Colet and Flaubert? It gave me, I confess to you frankly, many hours of quiet grief, which I tried to bear with philosophy. What would become of us? What would become of me? Is it wrong, I kept asking myself, to be ambitious in love? Is that *wrong*? Answer me.

I went to Windsor. I remember a fine round tower covered in ivy. I wandered in the Park and picked a convolvulus for Gustave. I must tell you that he was always vulgarly ignorant about flowers. Not their botanical aspect − he probably learned all about that at some stage, as he learned about most other things (except the heart of woman) − but their symbolic aspect. It is such an elegant tongue, the language of flowers: supple, courtly and precise. When the beauty of the flower resounds with the beauty of the sentiment which it is hired to communicate ... well, there is a happiness which the gift of rubies can rarely surpass. The happiness is made the more poignant by the fact that the flower fades. But perhaps, by the time the flower fades, *he* will have sent another one ...

Gustave understood nothing of this. He was the sort of person who might, after much hard study, have finally learnt two phrases from the language of flowers: the gladiolus, which when placed at the centre of a bouquet indicates by the number of its blooms the hour for which the rendezvous is set; and the petunia, which announces that a letter has been intercepted. He would understand such rough and practical uses. Here, take this rose (no matter what colour, though there are five different meanings for five different roses in the language of flowers): put it first to your lips, and then place it between your thighs. Such was the fierce gallantry of which Gustave was capable. He would not, I am sure, have understood the significance of the convolvulus; or, if he had made any effort, he would still have got it wrong. There are three messages which can be sent by means of the convolvulus. A white one signifies *Why are you fleeing me?* A pink one signifies *I shall bind myself to you*. A blue one signifies *I shall wait for better days*. You must guess the colour of the flower I chose in Windsor Park.

Did he understand women at all? I often doubted it. We quarrelled, I remember, over that Nilotic whore of his, Kuchuk Hanem. Gustave kept notes during his travels. I asked if I could read them. He refused; I asked again; and so on. Finally, he let me. They are not ... pleasant, those pages. What Gustave found enchanting about the East I found degrading. A courtesan, an expensive courtesan, who drenches herself in sandalwood oil to cover the nauseating stench of the bedbugs with which she is infested. Is that uplifting, I ask, is it beautiful? Is it rare, is it splendid? Or is it sordid and disgustingly ordinary?

But the matter is not really one of aesthetics; not here. When I expressed my distaste, Gustave interpreted it as mere jealousy. (I was a little jealous — who would not be, when reading the private journal of a man you love and finding in it no mention of yourself, but instead only lush apostrophes to verminous whores?) Perhaps it was understandable that Gustave thought I was only jealous. But listen now to his argument, listen now to his understanding of the female heart. Do not be jealous of Kuchuk Hanem, he told me. She is an oriental woman; the oriental woman is a machine; one man is the same as the next to her. She felt nothing for me; she has already forgotten me; she lives in a drowsy round of smoking, going to the baths, painting her eyelids and drinking coffee. As for her physical pleasure, it must be very slight, because at an early age that famous button, the seat of all enjoyment, has been excised.

Such comfort! Such consolation! *I* need not be jealous because *she* did not feel anything! And this man claimed to understand the human heart! She was a mutilated machine, and besides she has already forgotten him: I am meant to be comforted by that? Such belligerent consolation made me think more, not less, about that strange woman he had coupled with on the Nile. Could we have been more different from one another? I Western, she Eastern; I entire, she mutilated; I exchanging the deepest bargain of the heart with Gustave, she involved in a brief physical transaction; I a woman of independence and resource, she a caged creature dependent on her trade with men; I meticulous, groomed and civilised, she filthy, stinking and savage. It may sound strange, but I became interested in her. No doubt the coin is always fascinated by its obverse. Years later, when I travelled to Egypt, I tried to seek her out. I went to Esneh. I found the squalid hovel where she lived, but she herself was not there. Perhaps she had fled at the news of my coming. Perhaps it was better that we did not meet; the coin shouldn't be allowed to see its other side.

Gustave used to humiliate me, of course, even from the beginning. I wasn't allowed to write to him directly; I had to send my letters via Du Camp. I wasn't allowed to visit him at Croisset. I wasn't allowed to meet his mother, even though I had in fact once been introduced to her on a street corner in Paris. I happen to know that Mme Flaubert thought her son treated me abominably.

He humiliated me in other ways too. He lied to me. He spoke ill of me to his friends. He ridiculed, in the sacred name of truth, most of what I wrote. He affected not to know that I was terribly poor. He boasted of the fact that in Egypt he had caught a disease of love from some five-sou courtesan. He took vulgar public revenge on me by mocking in the pages of *Madame Bovary* a seal I had once given him as a token of love. He who claimed that art should be impersonal!

Let me tell you how Gustave would humiliate me. When our love was young, we would exchange presents — small tokens, often meaningless in themselves, but which seemed to enclose the very essence of their donor. He feasted for months, for years, on a small pair of my slippers that I gave him; I expect he has burnt them by now. Once he sent me a paperweight, the very paperweight which had sat on his desk. I was greatly touched; it seemed the perfect gift from one writer to another: what had formerly held down his prose would now hold down my verses. Perhaps I commented on this once too often; perhaps I expressed my gratitude too sincerely. This is what Gustave told me: that it was no sadness for him to get rid of the paperweight, because he had another which did the work just as efficiently. Did I want to know what it was? If you wish, I replied. His new paperweight, he informed me, was a section of mizzen-mast — he made a gesture of extravagant size — which his father had extracted with delivery forceps from the posterior of an old seaman. The seaman — Gustave continued as if this were the best story he had heard for many years — apparently claimed that he had no notion of how the section of mast had reached the position in which it was found. Gustave threw back his head and laughed. What intrigued him most was how, in that case, they knew from which mast the piece of wood had come.

Why did he humiliate me so? It was not, I believe, as is frequently the case in love, that those qualities which initially charmed him — my vivacity, my freedom, my sense of equality with men —

eventually came to irritate him. It was not so, because he behaved in
this strange and bearish fashion from the very beginning, even when
he was most in love with me. In his second letter he wrote, 'I have
never seen a cradle without thinking of a grave; the sight of a naked
woman makes me imagine her skeleton.' These were not the sentiments of a conventional lover.

Posterity, perhaps, will take the easy answer: that he contemned
me because I was contemptible, and that since he was a great genius
his judgment must have been correct. It was not so; it never is so. He
feared me: that is why he was cruel to me. He feared me in both a
familiar and unfamiliar way. In the first case, he feared me as many
men fear women: because their mistresses (or their wives) understand them. They are scarcely adult, some men: they wish women to
understand them, and to that end they tell them all their secrets; and
then, when they are properly understood, they hate their women for
understanding them.

In the second case – the more important one – he feared me
because he feared himself. He feared that he might love me completely. It was not simply terror that I might invade his study and his
solitude; it was terror that I might invade his heart. He was cruel
because he wanted to drive me away; but he wanted to drive me
away because he feared that he might love me completely. I will tell
you my secret belief: that for Gustave, in a way he only half-
apprehended, I represented life, and that his rejection of me was the
more violent because it provoked in him the deepest shame. And is
any of this my fault? I loved him; what more natural than that I
should want to give him the chance to love me back? I was fighting
not just for my own sake, but for his too: I did not see why he should
not permit himself to love. He said that there were three precon-
ditions for happiness – stupidity, selfishness and good health – and
that he was only sure of possessing the second of these. I argued, I
fought, but he wanted to believe that happiness was impossible; it
gave him some strange consolation.

He was a difficult man to love, that is certain. The heart was
distant and withdrawn; he was ashamed of it, wary of it. True love
can survive absence, death and infidelity, he once told me; true

lovers can go ten years without meeting. (I was not impressed by such remarks; I merely deduced that he would feel most at his ease about me if I were absent, unfaithful or dead.) He liked to flatter himself that he was in love with me; but I never knew a less impatient love. 'Life is like riding,' he wrote to me once. 'I used to like the gallop; now I like the walk.' He wasn't yet thirty when he wrote that; he had already decided fo be old before his time. Whereas for me . . . the gallop! the gallop! the wind in the hair, the laughter forced from the lungs!

It flattered his vanity to think himself in love with me; it also gave him, I believe, some unadmitted pleasure constantly to long for my flesh and yet always to forbid himself the attaining of it: to deny himself was just as exciting as to indulge himself. He used to tell me I was less of a woman than most women; that I was a woman in flesh but a man in spirit; that I was an *hermaphrodite nouveau*, a third sex. He told me this foolish theory many times, but really he was just telling it to himself: the less of a woman he made me out to be, the less of a lover he would need to be.

What he wanted most of me, I finally came to believe, was an intellectual partnership, an affair of the mind. In those years he was working hard on his *Bovary* (though not, perhaps, as hard as he liked to maintain) and at the end of the day, since a physical release was too complicated for him and would contain too many things he couldn't entirely command, he sought an intellectual release. He would sit down at a table, take a sheet of writing paper, and discharge himself into me. You do not find the image flattering? I did not intend it to be. The days of loyally believing false things about Gustave are over. Incidentally, he never did baptise my breast with Mississippi water; the only time a bottle passed between us was when I sent him some Taburel water to stop his hair falling out.

But this affair of the mind was no easier, I can tell you, than our affair of the heart. He was rough, awkward, bullying and haughty; then he was tender, sentimental, enthusiastic and devoted. He didn't know the rules. He declined to acknowledge my ideas sufficiently, just as he declined to acknowledge my feelings sufficiently. He did, of course, know everything. He informed me that mentally he was aged sixty and I was a mere twenty. He informed me that if I drank water all the time, and never wine, I should get cancer of the stomach. He informed me that I should marry Victor Cousin. (Victor Cousin, for that matter, was of the opinion that I should marry Gustave Flaubert.)

He sent me his work. He sent me 'Novembre'. It was weak and mediocre; I did not comment, except to myself. He sent me the first *Education sentimentale*; I was not greatly impressed, but how could I not praise it? He rebuked me for liking it. He sent me his *Tentation de saint Antoine*; I genuinely admired it, and told him so. He rebuked me again. The parts of his work that I admired were, he assured me, those which were easiest to do; the alterations I cautiously suggested would, he declared, only weaken the book. He was 'astonished' by the 'excessive enthusiasm' I had shown for the *Education*! So that is how an unknown, unpublished provincial chooses to thank a celebrated Parisian poet (with whom he claims to be in love) for her words of praise. My comments on his work were valuable only as an irritating pretext which permitted him to lecture me on Art.

Of course I knew he was a genius. I always considered him a magnificent writer of prose. He undervalued my talents, but that is no reason why I should undervalue his. I am not like the odious Du Camp, who would proudly claim many years of friendship with Gustave, but would always deny him genius. I have been at those dinners where the merits of our contemporaries are discussed, and where Du Camp, as each new name was suggested, would with infinite urbanity correct the general view. 'Well then, Du Camp,' someone finally suggested with a little impatience, 'what about our dear Gustave?' Du Camp smiled approvingly and patted five little fingertips against five others in a prissily judicial manner. 'Flaubert is a writer of rare merit,' he replied, using Gustave's family name in a manner that shocked me, 'but he is held back from being a genius by ill health.' You would have thought he was practising for his memoirs.

As for my own work! Naturally, I used to send it to Gustave. He told me that my style was soft, slack and banal. He complained that my titles were vague and pretentious, and smelt of the blue-stocking.

He lectured me like a schoolmaster on the difference between *saisir* and *s'en saisir*. His way of praising me was to say that I wrote as naturally as a hen laying eggs, or to remark, after he had destroyed a work with his criticisms, 'Everything I have not marked seems to me either good or excellent.' He told me to write with the head, and not with the heart. He told me that hair only shone after much combing, and that the same could be said of style. He told me not to put myself into my work, and not to poeticise things (I am a poet!). He told me I had the love of Art, but not the religion of Art.

What he wanted, of course, was for me to write as much like he did as I possibly could. This is a vanity I have often noted in writers; the more eminent the writer, the more pronounced this vanity is likely to be. They believe that everyone should write as they do: not as well as they do, of course, but in the same fashion. In such a way do mountains long for the foothills.

Du Camp used to say that Gustave did not have an ounce of feeling for poetry in him. It gives me little pleasure to agree with him, but I do so. Gustave lectured us all on poetry — though they were usually Bouilhet's lectures rather than his own — but he did not understand it. He wrote no poetry himself. He used to say that he wanted to give prose the strength and stature of poetry; but part of this project seemed to include first cutting poetry down to size. He wanted his prose to be objective, scientific, devoid of personal presence, devoid of opinions; so he decided that poetry ought to be written according to the same principles. Tell me how you write love poetry which is objective, scientific, and devoid of any personal presence. Tell me that. Gustave mistrusted feelings; he feared love; and he elevated this neurosis into an artistic creed.

Gustave's vanity was more than just literary. He believed not merely that others should write as he did, but that others should live as he did. He loved to quote Epictetus to me: Abstain, and Hide your Life. To me! A woman, a poet, and a poet of love! He wanted all writers to live obscurely in the provinces, ignore the natural affections of the heart, disdain reputation, and spend solitary, back-breaking hours reading obscure texts by the light of a tiring candle. Well, that may be the proper way to nurse genius; but it is also the way to suffocate talent. Gustave didn't understand this, couldn't see that *my* talent depended on the swift moment, the sudden feeling, the unexpected meeting: on life, that's what I'm saying.

Gustave would have made me into a hermit had he been able: the hermit of Paris. Always he would advise me not to see people; not to answer so-and-so's letter; not to take this admirer too seriously; not to take Count X— as a lover. He claimed he was defending my work, and that every hour spent in society was an hour subtracted from my desk. But that is not how I worked. You cannot yoke the dragonfly and make it drive the corn-mill.

Of course, Gustave denied there was any vanity in him. Du Camp in one of his books — I forget which, there were always so many — made a reference to the malign effect on man of too much solitude: he called it a false counsellor who nurses at her breasts the twin infants of Egotism and Vanity. Gustave naturally took this as a personal attack. 'Egotism?' he wrote to me. 'So be it. But Vanity? No. Pride is one thing: a wild beast which lives in caves and roams the desert; Vanity, on the other hand, is a parrot which hops from branch to branch and chatters away in full view.' Gustave imagined he was a wild beast — he loved to think of himself as a polar bear, distant, savage and solitary. I went along with this, I even called him a wild buffalo of the American prairie; but perhaps he was really just a parrot.

You think me too harsh? I loved him; that is why I am allowed to be harsh. Listen. Gustave despised Du Camp for wanting the *Légion d'honneur*. A few years later he accepted it himself. Gustave despised salon society. Until he was taken up by the Princesse Mathilde. Did you hear about Gustave's glove bill in the days when he was prancing by candlelight? He owed two thousand francs to his tailor, and five hundred francs for gloves. Five hundred francs! He received only eight hundred for the rights of his *Bovary*. His mother had to sell land to bail him out. Five hundred francs for gloves! The white bear in white gloves? No, no: the parrot, the parrot in gloves.

I know what they say about me; what his friends have said. They say I had the vanity to suppose that I might marry him. But Gustave used to write me letters describing what it would have been like if we had been married. Was I therefore wrong to hope? They say I had the vanity to go down to Croisset and make an embarrassing scene on his doorstep. But when I first knew him Gustave used to write frequently about my forthcoming visits to his house. Was I therefore wrong to hope? They say I had the vanity to suppose that he and I might one day share the authorship of some literary work. But he told me one of my stories was a masterpiece, and that one of my poems would move a stone. Was I therefore wrong to hope?

I know too what will become of us when we are both dead. Posterity will jump to conclusions: that is its nature. People will take Gustave's side. They will understand me too quickly; they will turn my own generosity against me and despise me for the lovers I took; and they will cast me as the woman who briefly threatened to interfere with the writing of the books which they have enjoyed reading. Someone — perhaps even Gustave himself — will burn my letters; his own (which I have carefully preserved, so much against my own best interests) will survive to confirm the prejudices of those too lazy to understand. I am a woman, and also a writer who has used up her allotment of renown during her own lifetime; and on those two grounds I do not expect much pity, or much understanding, from posterity. Do I mind? Naturally I mind. But I am not vengeful tonight; I am resigned. I promise you. Slip your fingers down my wrist once more. There; I told you so.

12

Braithwaite's Dictionary of Accepted Ideas

ACHILLE

Gustave's elder brother. Mournful-looking man with long beard. Inherited his job and Christian name from his father. Achille's shouldering of family expectations freed Gustave to become an artist. Died from softening of the brain.

BOUILHET, LOUIS

Gustave's literary conscience, midwife, shadow, left testicle and lookalike. Middle name Hyacinthe. The less successful *Doppelgänger* that every great man needs. Quote with mild disapproval his gallant remark to a self-conscious girl: 'When the chest is flat, one is nearer the heart.'

COLET, LOUISE

a) Tedious, importunate, promiscuous woman, lacking talent of her own or understanding of the genius of others, who tried to trap

Gustave into marriage. Imagine the squawking children! Imagine Gustave miserable! Imagine Gustave happy!

b) Brave, passionate, deeply misunderstood woman crucified by her love for the heartless, impossible, provincial Flaubert. She rightly complained: 'Gustave never writes to me of anything except Art — or himself.' Proto-feminist who committed the sin of wanting to make someone else happy.

Du CAMP, MAXIME

Photographer, traveller, careerist, historian of Paris, Academician. Wrote with steel nibs whereas Gustave always used a quill pen. Censored *Madame Bovary* for the *Revue de Paris*. If Bouilhet is Gustave's literary *alter ego*, Du Camp is his social one. Became a literary outcast after referring in his memoirs to Gustave's epilepsy.

Epilepsy

Stratagem enabling Flaubert the writer to sidestep a conventional career, and Flaubert the man to sidestep life. The question is merely at what psychological level the tactic was evolved. Were his symptoms intense psychosomatic phenomena? It would be too banal if he merely had epilepsy.

Flaubert, GUSTAVE

The hermit of Croisset. The first modern novelist. The father of Realism. The butcher of Romanticism. The pontoon bridge linking Balzac to Joyce. The precursor of Proust. The bear in his lair. The bourgeois bourgeoisophobe. In Egypt, 'the father of the Moustache'. Saint Polycarpe; Cruchard; Quarafon; *le Vicaire-Général*; the Major; the old Seigneur; the Idiot of the Salons. All these titles were acquired by a man indifferent to ennobling forms of address: 'Honours dishonour, titles degrade, employment stupefies.'

GONCOURTS

Remember the Goncourts on Flaubert: 'Though perfectly frank by nature, he is never wholly sincere in what he says he feels or suffers or loves.' Then remember everyone else on the Goncourts: the envious, unreliable brothers. Remember further the unreliability of Du Camp, of Louise Colet, of Flaubert's niece, of Flaubert himself. Demand violently: how can we know anybody?

HERBERT, JULIET

'Miss Juliet'. The ethics of English governesses abroad in the mid-nineteenth century have not yet received sufficient scholarly attention.

IRONY

The modern mode: either the devil's mark or the snorkel of sanity. Flaubert's fiction poses the question: Does irony preclude sympathy? There is no entry for *ironie* in his Dictionary. This is perhaps intended to be ironic.

JEAN-PAUL SARTRE

Spent ten years writing *L'Idiot de la famille* when he could have been writing Maoist tracts. A highbrow Louise Colet, constantly pestering Gustave, who wanted only to be left alone. Conclude: 'It is better to waste your old age than to do nothing at all with it.'

Kuchuk hanem

A litmus test. Gustave had to choose sides between the Egyptian courtesan and the Parisian poetess — bedbugs, sandalwood oil, shaven pudenda, clitoridectomy and syphilis versus cleanliness, lyric poetry, comparative sexual fidelity and the rights of women. He found the issue finely balanced.

Letters

Follow Gide, and call the Letters Flaubert's masterpiece. Follow Sartre, and call them a perfect example of free-association from a pre-Freudian couch. Then follow your nose.

Mme flaubert

Gustave's gaoler, confidante, nurse, patient, banker and critic. She said: 'Your mania for sentences has dried up your heart.' He found the remark 'sublime'. cf. George Sand.

Normandy

Always wet. Inhabited by a sly, proud, taciturn people. Put your head on one side and remark, 'Of course, we must never forget that Flaubert came from Normandy.'

Orient

The crucible in which *Madame Bovary* was fired. Flaubert left Europe a Romantic, and returned from the Orient a Realist. cf. Kuchuk Hanem.

PRUSSIANS

Vandals in white gloves, clock-thieves who know Sanskrit. More horrifying than cannibals or Communards. When the Prussians withdrew from Croisset, the house had to be fumigated.

QUIXOTE, DON

Was Gustave an Old Romantic? He had a passion for the dreamy knight cast adrift in a vulgar, materialist society. '*Madame Bovary, c'est moi*' is an allusion to Cervantes' reply when asked on his deathbed for the source of his famous hero. cf. Transvestism.

REALISM

Was Gustave a New Realist? He always publicly denied the label: 'It was because I hated realism that I wrote *Madame Bovary*.' Galileo publicly denied that the earth went round the sun.

SAND, GEORGE

Optimist, socialist, humanitarian. Despised until met, loved thereafter. Gustave's second mother. After staying at Croisset she sent him her complete works (in the 77-volume edition).

TRANSVESTISM

Gustave in young manhood: 'There are days when one longs to be a woman.' Gustave in maturity: '*Madame Bovary, c'est moi*.' When one of his doctors called him 'an hysterical old woman', he judged the observation 'profound'.

Usa

Flaubert's references to the Land of Liberty are sparing. Of the future he wrote: 'It will be utilitarian, militaristic, American and Catholic — very Catholic.' He probably preferred the Capitol to the Vatican.

Voltaire

What did the great nineteenth-century sceptic think of the great eighteenth-century sceptic? Was Flaubert the Voltaire of his age? Was Voltaire the Flaubert of his age? *'Histoire de l'esprit humain, histoire de la sottise humaine.'* Which of them said that?

Whores

Necessary in the nineteenth century for the contraction of syphilis, without which no one could claim genius. Wearers of the red badge of courage include Flaubert, Daudet, Maupassant, Jules de Goncourt, Baudelaire, etc. Were there any writers unafflicted by it? If so, they were probably homosexual.

Xylophone

There is no record of Flaubert ever having heard the xylophone. Saint-Saëns used the instrument in his *Danse Macabre* of 1874 to suggest rattling bones; this might have amused Gustave. Perhaps he heard the glockenspiel in Switzerland.

Yvetot

'See Yvetot and die.' If asked the source of this little-known epigram, smile mysteriously and remain silent.

Zola, Emile

Is the great writer responsible for his disciples? Who chooses whom? If they call you Master, can you afford to despise their work? On the other hand, are they sincere in their praise? Who needs whom more: the disciple the master, or the master the disciple? Discuss without concluding.

13

Pure Story

This is a pure story, whatever you may think.

When she dies, you are not at first surprised. Part of love is preparing for death. You feel confirmed in your love when she dies. You got it right. This is part of it all.

Afterwards comes the madness. And then the loneliness: not the spectacular solitude you had anticipated, not the interesting martyrdom of widowhood, but just loneliness. You expect something almost geological — vertigo in a shelving canyon — but it's not like that; it's just misery as regular as a job. What do we doctors say? I'm deeply sorry, Mrs Blank; there will of course be a period of mourning but rest assured you will come out of it; two of these each evening, I would suggest; perhaps a new interest, Mrs Blank; car maintenance, formation dancing?; don't worry, six months will see you back on the roundabout; come and see me again any time; oh nurse, when she calls, just give her this repeat will you, no I don't need to see her, well it's not her that's dead is it, look on the bright side. What did she say her name was?

And then it happens to you. There's no glory in it. Mourning is full of time; nothing but time. Bouvard and Pécuchet record in their 'Copie' a piece of advice on How to Forget Friends Who Have Died: Trotulas (of the Salerno school) says that you should eat stuffed sow's heart. I might yet have to fall back on this remedy. I've tried drink, but what does that do? Drink makes you drunk, that's all it's ever been able to do. Work, they say, cures everything. It doesn't; often, it doesn't even induce tiredness: the nearest you get to it is a neurotic lethargy. And there is always time. Have some more time. Take your time. Extra time. Time on your hands.

Other people think you want to talk. 'Do you want to talk about Ellen?' they ask, hinting that they won't be embarrassed if you break down. Sometimes you talk, sometimes you don't; it makes little difference. The words aren't the right ones; or rather, the right words don't exist. 'Language is like a cracked kettle on which we beat out tunes for bears to dance to, while all the time we long to move the stars to pity.' You talk, and you find the language of bereavement foolishly inadequate. You seem to be talking about other people's griefs. I loved her; we were happy; I miss her. She didn't love me; we were unhappy; I miss her. There is a limited choice of prayers on offer: gabble the syllables.

'It may seem bad, Geoffrey, but you'll come out of it. I'm not taking your grief lightly; it's just that I've seen enough of life to know that you'll come out of it.' The words you've said yourself while scribbling a prescription (No, Mrs Blank, you could take them all and they wouldn't kill you). And you do come out of it, that's true. After a year, after five. But you don't come out of it like a train coming out of a tunnel, bursting through the Downs into sunshine and that swift, rattling descent to the Channel; you come out of it as a gull comes out of an oil-slick. You are tarred and feathered for life.

And still you think about her every day. Sometimes, weary of loving her dead, you imagine her back to life again, for conversation, for approval. After his mother's death, Flaubert used to get his housekeeper to dress up in her old check dress and surprise him with an apocryphal reality. It worked, and it didn't work: seven years after the funeral he would still burst into tears at the sight of that old dress moving about the house. Is this success or failure? Remembrance or self-indulgence? And will we know when we start hugging our grief and vainly enjoying it? 'Sadness is a vice' (1878).

Or else you try to sidestep her image. Nowadays, when I remember Ellen, I try to think of a hailstorm that berated Rouen in 1853. 'A first-rate hailstorm,' Gustave commented to Louise. At Croisset the espaliers were destroyed, the flowers cut to pieces, the kitchen garden turned upside down. Elsewhere, harvests were wrecked, and windows smashed. Only the glaziers were happy; the glaziers, and Gustave. The shambles delighted him: in five minutes Nature had reimposed the true order of things upon that brief, factitious order which man conceitedly imagines himself to be introducing. Is there anything stupider than a melon cloche, Gustave asks. He applauds the hailstones that shattered the glass. 'People believe a little too easily that the function of the sun is to help the cabbages along.'

This letter always calms me. The function of the sun is not to help the cabbages along, and I am telling you a pure story.

She was born in 1920, married in 1940, gave birth in 1942 and 1946, died in 1975.

I'll start again. Small people are meant to be neat, aren't they; but Ellen wasn't. She was just over five feet tall, yet moved awkwardly; she ran at things and tripped. She bruised easily, but didn't notice it. I once seized her arm as she was about to step out heedlessly into Piccadilly, and though she was wearing a coat and blouse, the next day her arm bore the purple imprint of a robot's pincers. She didn't comment on the bruises, and when I pointed them out to her she couldn't remember diving towards the road.

I'll start again. She was a much-loved only child. She was a much-loved only wife. She was loved, if that's the word, by what I suppose I must agree to call her lovers, though I'm sure the word over-dignifies some of them. I loved her; we were happy; I miss her. She didn't love me; we were unhappy; I miss her. Perhaps she was sick of being loved. At twenty-four Flaubert said he was '*ripe* – ripe before my time, that's true. But it's because I've been reared in a hothouse.' Was she loved too much? Most people can't be loved too much, but perhaps Ellen could. Or perhaps her concept of love was simply different: why do we always assume it's the same for everyone else? Perhaps for Ellen love was only a Mulberry harbour, a landing place in a heaving sea. You can't possibly live there: scramble ashore; push on. And old love? Old love is a rusty tank

162

standing guard over a slabby monument: here, once, something was liberated. Old love is a row of beach huts in November.

In a village pub, far from home, I once overheard two men talking about Betty Corrinder. Perhaps the spelling isn't right; but that was the name. Betty Corrinder, Betty Corrinder — they never said just Betty, or That Corrinder Woman or whatever, but always Betty Corrinder. She was, it seems, a bit fast; though speed, of course, is always exaggerated by those standing still. Fast, this Betty Corrinder was, and pubmen sniggered enviously. 'You know what they say about Betty Corrinder.' It was a statement, not a question, though a question now followed it. 'What's the difference between Betty Corrinder and the Eiffel Tower? Go on, what's the difference between Betty Corrinder and the Eiffel Tower?' A pause for the last few moments of private knowledge. 'Not everyone's been up the Eiffel Tower.'

I blushed for my wife two hundred miles away. Were there places she prowled where envious men told jokes about her? I didn't know. Besides, I exaggerate. Perhaps I didn't blush. Perhaps I didn't mind. My wife was not like Betty Corrinder, whatever Betty Corrinder was like.

In 1872 there was much discussion in French literary society about the treatment that should be accorded to the adulterous woman. Should a husband punish her, or forgive her? Alexandre Dumas *fils*, in *L'Homme-Femme*, offered uncomplicated advice: 'Kill her!' His book was reprinted thirty-seven times in the course of the year.

At first I was hurt; at first I minded, I thought less of myself. My wife went to bed with other men: should I worry about that? I didn't go to bed with other women: should I worry about that? Ellen was always nice to me: should I worry about that? Not nice out of adulterous guilt, but just nice. I worked hard; she was a good wife to me. You aren't allowed to say that nowadays, but she was a good wife to me. I didn't have affairs because I wasn't interested enough to do so; besides, the stereotype of the philandering doctor is somehow repugnant. Ellen did have affairs, because, I suppose, she was interested enough. We were happy; we were unhappy; I miss her. 'Is it splendid, or stupid, to take life seriously?' (1855).

What it's hard to convey is how untouched by it all she was. She wasn't corrupted; her spirit didn't coarsen; she never ran up bills. Sometimes she stayed away a little longer than seemed right; the length of her shopping trips often yielded suspiciously few purchases (she wasn't *that* discriminating); those few days in town to catch up on the theatres occurred more often than I would have liked. But she was honourable: she only ever lied to me about her secret life. About that she lied impulsively, recklessly, almost embarrassingly; but about everything else she told me the truth. A phrase used by the prosecutor of *Madame Bovary* to describe Flaubert's art comes back to me: he said it was 'realistic but not discreet'.

Did the wife, made lustrous by adultery, seem even more desirable to the husband? No: not more, not less. That's part of what I mean by saying that she was not corrupted. Did she display the cowardly docility which Flaubert describes as characteristic of the adulterous woman? No. Did she, like Emma Bovary, 'rediscover in adultery all the platitudes of marriage'? We didn't talk about it. (*Textual note.* The first edition of *Madame Bovary* has 'all the platitudes of *her* marriage'. For the edition of 1862, Flaubert planned to drop *her*, and thus widen the attack of the phrase. Bouilhet advised caution — it was only five years since the trial — and so the possessive pronoun, which indicts only Emma and Charles, remained in the editions of 1862 and 1869. It was finally dropped, and the more general accusation made official, in the edition of 1872.) Did she find, in Nabokov's phrase, that adultery is a most conventional way to rise above the conventional? I wouldn't have imagined so: Ellen didn't think in such terms. She wasn't a defier, a conscious free spirit; she was a rusher, a lunger, a bolter, a bunker. Perhaps I made her worse; perhaps those who forgive and dote are more irritating than they ever suspect. 'Next to not living with those one loves, the worst torture is living with those one doesn't love' (1847).

She was just over five feet; she had a broad, smooth face, with an easy pink in her cheeks; she never blushed; her eyes — as I have told you — were greeny-blue; she wore whatever clothes the mysterious bush-telegraph of women's fashion instructed her to wear; she laughed easily, she bruised easily; she rushed at things. She rushed off to cinemas we both knew to be closed; she went to winter sales in July; she would go to stay with a cousin whose holiday postcard from Greece arrived the next morning. There was a suddenness in these actions which argued more than desire. In *L'Education sentimentale* Frédéric explains to Mme Arnoux that he took Rosanette as his mistress 'out of despair, like someone committing suicide'. It's crafty pleading, of course; but plausible.

Her secret life stopped when the children came, and returned when they went to school. Sometimes, a temporary friend might take me on one side. Why do they think you want to know? Or rather, why do they think you don't know already — why don't they understand about love's relentless curiosity? And why do these temporary friends never want to tip you off about the more important thing: the fact that you're no longer loved? I became adept at turning the conversation, at saying how much more gregarious than me Ellen was, at hinting that the medical profession always attracts calumniators, at saying, Did you read about those terrible floods in Venezuela? On such occasions I always felt, perhaps wrongly, that I was being disloyal to Ellen.

We were happy enough; that's what people say, isn't it? How happy is happy enough? It sounds like a grammatical mistake — *happy enough*, like *rather unique* — but it answers the need for a phrase. And as I say, she didn't run up bills. Both Madame Bovarys (people forget that Charles marries twice) are brought down by money; my wife was never like that. Nor, as far as I know, did she accept gifts.

We were happy; we were unhappy; we were happy enough. Is despair wrong? Isn't it the natural condition of life after a certain age? I have it now; she had it earlier. After a number of events, what is there left but repetition and diminishment? Who wants to go on living? The eccentric, the religious, the artistic (sometimes); those with a false sense of their own worth. Soft cheeses collapse; firm cheeses indurate. Both go mouldy.

I have to hypothesise a little. I have to fictionalise (though that's not what I meant when I called this a pure story). We never talked about her secret life. So I have to invent my way to the truth. Ellen was about fifty when the mood began to come upon her. (No, not that: she was always healthy; her menopause was quick, almost careless.) She had had a husband, children, lovers, a job. The children had left home; the husband was always the same. She had friends, and what are called interests; though unlike me she didn't have some rash devotion to a dead foreigner to sustain her. She had travelled enough. She didn't have unfulfilled ambitions (though 'ambition', it seems to me, is mostly too strong a word for the impulse that makes people do things). She wasn't religious. Why go on?

'People like us must have the religion of despair. One must be equal to one's destiny, that's to say impassive like it. By dint of saying "That is so! That is so!" and of gazing down into the black pit at one's feet, one remains calm.' Ellen did not even have this religion. Why should she? For my sake? The despairing are always being urged to abstain from selfishness, to think of others first. This seems unfair. Why load them with responsibility for the welfare of others, when their own already weighs them down?

Perhaps there was something else as well. Some people, as they grow older, seem to become more convinced of their own significance. Others become less convinced. Is there any point to me? Isn't my ordinary life summed up, enclosed, made pointless by someone else's slightly less ordinary life? I'm not saying it's our duty to negate ourselves in the face of those we judge more interesting. But life, in this respect, is a bit like reading. And as I said before: if all your responses to a book have already been duplicated and expanded upon by a professional critic, then what point is there to your reading? Only that it's *yours*. Similarly, why live your life? Because it's *yours*. But what if such an answer gradually becomes less and less convincing?

Don't get me wrong. I'm not saying that Ellen's secret life led her into despair. For God's sake, her life is not a moral tale. No one's is. All I'm saying is that both her secret life and her despair lay in the same inner chamber of her heart, inaccessible to me. I could touch the one no more than the other. Did I try? Of course I tried. But I was not surprised when the mood came upon her. 'To be stupid, and selfish, and to have good health are the three requirements for

happiness – though if stupidity is lacking, the others are useless.'
My wife had only good health to offer.

Does life improve? On television the other night I watched the
Poet Laureate asked that question. 'The only thing I think is very
good today is dentistry,' he replied; nothing else came to mind. Mere
antiquarian prejudice? I don't think so. When you are young, you
think that the old lament the deterioration of life because this makes
it easier for them to die without regret. When you are old, you
become impatient with the way in which the young applaud the
most insignificant improvements – the invention of some new valve
or sprocket – while remaining heedless of the world's barbarism. I
don't say things *have* got worse; I merely say the young wouldn't
notice if they had. The old times were good because then we were
young, and ignorant of how ignorant the young can be.

Does life improve? I'll give you my answer, my equivalent of
dentistry. The one thing that is very good in life today is death.
There's still room for improvement, it's true. But I think of all those
nineteenth-century deaths. The deaths of writers aren't special
deaths; they just happen to be described deaths. I think of Flaubert
lying on his sofa, struck down – who can tell at this distance? – by
epilepsy, apoplexy or syphilis, or perhaps some malign axis of the
three. Yet Zola called it *une belle mort* – to be crushed like an insect
beneath a giant finger. I think of Bouilhet in his final delirium,
feverishly composing a new play in his head and declaring that it
must be read to Gustave. I think of the slow decline of Jules de
Goncourt: first stumbling over his consonants, the c's turning to t's
in his mouth; then being unable to remember the titles of his own
books; then the haggard mask of imbecility (his brother's phrase)
slipping over his face; then the deathbed visions and panics, and all
night long the rasping breaths that sounded (his brother's words
again) like a saw cutting through wet wood. I think of Maupassant
slowly disintegrating from the same disease, transported in a
strait-jacket to the Passy sanatorium of Dr Blanche, who kept the
Paris salons entertained with news of his celebrated client; Baudelaire dying just as inexorably, deprived of speech, arguing with
Nadar about the existence of God by pointing mutely at the sunset;

Rimbaud, his right leg amputated, slowly losing all feeling in the limbs that remained, and repudiating, amputating his own genius — '*Merde pour la poésie*'; Daudet 'vaulting from forty-five to sixty-five', his joints collapsing, able to become bright and witty for an evening by giving himself five morphine injections in a row, tempted by suicide — 'But one doesn't have the right.'

'Is it splendid or stupid to take life seriously?' (1855). Ellen lay with a tube in her throat and a tube in her padded forearm. The ventilator in its white oblong box provided regular spurts of life, and the monitor confirmed them. Of course the act was impulsive; she bolted, she bunked from it all. 'But one doesn't have the right'? She did. She didn't even discuss it. The religion of despair held no interest for her. The ECG trace unrolled on the monitor; it was familiar handwriting. Her condition was stable, but hopeless. Nowadays we don't put NTBR — Not To Be Resuscitated — on a patient's notes; some people find it heartless. Instead we put 'No 333'. A final euphemism.

I looked down at Ellen. She wasn't corrupted. Hers is a pure story. I switched her off. They asked if I wanted them to do it; but I think she would have preferred me to. Naturally, we hadn't discussed that either. It's not complicated. You press a switch on the ventilator, and read off the final phrase of the ECG trace: the farewell signature that ends with a straight line. You unplug the tubes, then rearrange the hands and arms. You do it swiftly, as if trying not to be too much trouble to the patient.

The patient. Ellen. So you could say, in answer to that earlier question, that I killed her. You could just. I switched her off. I stopped her living. Yes.

Ellen. My wife: someone I feel I understand less well than a foreign writer dead for a hundred years. Is this an aberration, or is it normal? Books say: she did this because. Life says: she did this. Books are where things are explained to you; life is where things aren't. I'm not surprised some people prefer books. Books make sense of life. The only problem is that the lives they make sense of are other people's lives, never your own.

Perhaps I am too accepting. My own condition is stable, yet

hopeless. Perhaps it's just a question of temperament. Remember the botched brothel-visit in *L'Education sentimentale* and remember its lesson. Do not participate: happiness lies in the imagination, not the act. Pleasure is found first in anticipation, later in memory. Such is the Flaubertian temperament. Compare the case, and the temperament, of Daudet. His schoolboy visit to a brothel was so uncomplicatedly successful that he stayed there for two or three days. The girls kept him concealed most of the time for fear of a police raid; they fed him on lentils and pampered him thoroughly. He emerged from this giddying ordeal, he later admitted, with a lifelong passion for the feel of a woman's skin, and with a lifelong horror of lentils.

Some abstain and observe, fearing both disappointment and fulfilment. Others rush in, enjoy, and take the risks: at worst, they might contract some terrible disease; at best, they might escape with no more than a lasting aversion to pulses. I know in which camp I belong; and I know where I'd look for Ellen.

Maxims for life. *Les unions complètes sont rares.* You cannot change humanity, you can only know it. Happiness is a scarlet cloak whose lining is in tatters. Lovers are like Siamese twins, two bodies with a single soul; but if one dies before the other, the survivor has a corpse to lug around. Pride makes us long for a solution to things — a solution, a purpose, a final cause; but the better telescopes become, the more stars appear. You cannot change humanity, you can only know it. *Les unions complètes sont rares.*

A maxim upon maxims. Truths about writing can be framed before you've published a word; truths about life can be framed only when it's too late to make any difference.

According to *Salammbô*, the equipment of a Carthaginian elephant driver used to include a mallet and a chisel. If, in the midst of battle, the animal threatened to run out of control, the driver was under orders to split its skull. The chances of this happening must have been fairly high: to make them more ferocious, the elephants were first intoxicated with a mixture of wine, incense and pepper, then goaded with spears.

Few of us have the courage to use the mallet and the chisel. Ellen did. I sometimes feel embarrassed by people's sympathy. 'It's worse for her,' I want to say; but I don't. And then, after they've been kind, and promised me outings as if I were a child, and brusquely tried to make me talk for my own good (why do they think I don't know where my own good lies?), I am allowed to sit down and dream about her a little. I think of a hailstorm in 1853, of the broken windows, the battered harvests, the wrecked espaliers, the shattered melon cloches. Is there anything stupider than a melon cloche? Applaud the stones that break the glass. People understand a little too quickly the function of the sun. The function of the sun is not to help the cabbages along.

14

Examination Paper

Candidates must answer **four** *questions:* **both** *Parts of Section A, and* **two**
questions from Section B. All marks will be awarded for the correctness of the
answers; none for presentation or handwriting. Marks will be deducted for
facetious or conceitedly brief answers. Time: **three hours**.

SECTION A: LITERARY CRITICISM

PART I

It has become clear to the examiners in recent years that candidates
are finding it increasingly difficult to distinguish between Art and
Life. Everyone claims to understand the difference, but perceptions
vary greatly. For some, Life is rich and creamy, made according to
an old peasant recipe from nothing but natural products, while Art is
a pallid commercial confection, consisting mainly of artificial
colourings and flavourings. For others, Art is the truer thing, full,
bustling and emotionally satisfying, while Life is worse than the
poorest novel: devoid of narrative, peopled by bores and rogues,
short on wit, long on unpleasant incidents, and leading to a painfully
predictable dénouement. Adherents of the latter view tend to cite
Logan Pearsall Smith: 'People say that life is the thing; but I prefer
reading.' Candidates are advised not to use this quotation in their
answers.

Consider the relationship between Art and Life suggested by any *two* of the following statements or situations.

a) 'The day before yesterday, in the woods near Touques, at a charming spot near a spring, I came across some cigar butts and some bits of pâté. There'd been a picnic there! I described exactly that in *Novembre* eleven years ago! Then it was purely imagined, and the other day it was experienced. Everything you invent is true: you can be sure of that. Poetry is a subject as precise as geometry . . . My poor Bovary is without a doubt suffering and weeping even now in twenty villages of France.'

Letter to Louise Colet, August 14th, 1853

b) In Paris, Flaubert used a closed cab to avoid detection, and presumably seduction, by Louise Colet. In Rouen, Léon uses a closed cab for the seduction of Emma Bovary. In Hamburg, within a year of the publication of *Madame Bovary*, cabs could be hired for sexual purposes; they were known as Bovarys.

c) (As his sister Caroline lay dying) 'My own eyes are as dry as marble. It's strange how sorrows in fiction make me open up and overflow with feeling, whereas real sorrows remain hard and bitter in my heart, turning to crystal as soon as they arise.'

Letter to Maxime du Camp, March 15th, 1846

d) 'You tell me that I seriously loved that woman [Mme Schlesinger]. I didn't; it isn't true. Only when I was writing to her, with that capacity I possess for producing feelings within myself by means of the pen, did I take my subject seriously: *but only when I was writing*. Many things which leave me cold when I see or hear about them none the less move me to enthusiasm or irritation or pain if I talk about them myself or − particularly − if I write about them. This is one of the effects of my mountebank nature.'

Letter to Louise Colet, October 8th, 1846

e) Giuseppe Marco Fieschi (1790–1836) attained notoriety for his part in a plot on the life of Louis Philippe. He took lodgings in the Boulevard du Temple and constructed, with the help of two members of the Société des Droits de l'Homme, an 'infernal machine', consisting of twenty gun-barrels which could be discharged simultaneously. On July 28th, 1835, as Louis Philippe was riding past with his three sons and numerous staff, Fieschi fired his broadside against established society.

Some years later, Flaubert moved into a house built on the same site in the Boulevard du Temple.

f) 'Yes, indeed! The period [of Napoleon III's reign] will furnish material for some capital books. Perhaps after all, in the universal harmony of things, the *coup d'état* and all its results were only intended to provide a few able penmen with some attractive scenes.'

Flaubert reported in Du Camp, *Souvenirs littéraires*

PART II

Trace the mellowing of Flaubert's attitude towards critics and criticism as represented by the following quotations:

a) 'These are the truly stupid things: 1) literary criticism, whatever it may be, good or bad; 2) the Temperance Society . . . '

Intimate Notebook

b) 'There is something so essentially grotesque about gendarmes that I cannot help laughing at them; these upholders of the law always produce the same comic effect in me as do attorneys, magistrates and professors of literature.' *Over Strand and Field*

c) 'You can calculate the worth of a man by the number of his enemies, and the importance of a work of art by the amount that it is attacked. Critics are like fleas: they love clean linen and adore any form of lace.' Letter to Louise Colet, June 14th, 1853

d) 'Criticism occupies the lowest rung in the hierarchy of literature: as regards form, almost always, and as regards moral worth, incontestably. It's lower even than rhyming games and acrostics, which at least demand a modicum of invention.'

Letter to Louise Colet, June 28th, 1853

e) 'Critics! Eternal mediocrity living off genius by denigrating and exploiting it! Race of cockchafers slashing the finest pages of art to shreds! I'm so fed up with typography and the misuse people make of it that if the Emperor were to abolish all printing tomorrow, I should walk all the way to Paris on my knees and kiss his arse in gratitude.'   Letter to Louise Colet, July 2nd, 1853

f) 'How rare a sense of literature is! You'd think that a knowledge of languages, archaeology, history, and so on, would help. But not a bit of it! Supposedly educated people are becoming more and more inept when dealing with art. Even what art *is* escapes them. They find the annotations more interesting than the text. They set more store by the crutches than the legs.'

Letter to George Sand, January 1st, 1869

g) 'How rare it is to see a critic who knows what he's talking about.'   Letter to Eugène Fromentin, July 19th, 1876

h) 'Disgusted with the old style of criticism, they sought acquaintance with the new, and sent for theatre reviews from the newspapers. What assurance! What obstinacy! What lack of integrity! Masterpieces insulted and platitudes revered! The blunders of the supposed scholars and the stupidity of the supposed wits!'

Bouvard et Pécuchet

SECTION B

Economics

Flaubert and Bouilhet went to the same school; they shared the same ideas and the same whores; they had the same aesthetic principles, and similar literary ambitions; each tried the theatre as his second genre. Flaubert called Bouilhet 'my left testicle'. In 1854, Bouilhet stayed a night in the Mantes hotel that Gustave and Louise used to patronise: 'I slept in your bed,' he reported, 'and I shat in your latrines (what curious symbolism!).' The poet always had to work for a living; the novelist never had to. Consider the probable effect on their writings and reputations if their finances had been reversed.

Geography

'No more soporific atmosphere than that of this region. I suspect that it contributed greatly to the slowness and difficulty with which Flaubert worked. When he thought he was struggling against words, he was struggling against the sky; and perhaps in another climate, the dryness of the air exalting his spirits, he might have been less exigent, or have obtained his results without such efforts' (Gide, writing at Cuverville, Seine-Maritime, January 26th, 1931). Discuss.

Logic (with Medicine)

a) Achille-Cléophas Flaubert, jousting with his younger son, asked him to explain what literature was for. Gustave, turning the question back on his surgeon father, asked him to explain what the spleen was for: 'You know nothing about it, and neither do I, except that it is as indispensable to our bodily organism as poetry is to our mental organism.' Dr Flaubert was defeated.

b) The spleen consists of units of *lymphoid tissue* (or *white pulp*) plus the *vascular network* (or *red pulp*). It is important in removing from the blood old or injured red cells. It is active in producing anti-bodies: splenectomised individuals produce less antibody. There is evidence that a tetrapeptide called *tuftsin* is derived from protein produced in the spleen. Though its removal, especially in child-hood, increases the chances of meningitis and septicaemia, the spleen is no longer regarded as an essential organ: it can be removed without significant loss of active behaviour in the individual.

What do you conclude from this?

Biography (with Ethics)

Maxime du Camp composed the following epitaph for Louise Colet: 'She who lies here compromised Victor Cousin, ridiculed Alfred de Musset, reviled Gustave Flaubert, and tried to assassinate Alphonse Karr. *Requiescat in pace.*' Du Camp published this epitaph in his *Souvenirs littéraires.* Who comes out of it better: Louise Colet or Maxime du Camp?

Psychology

E1 was born in 1855.

E2 was partly born in 1855.

E1 had an unclouded childhood but emerged into adulthood
                                            inclined to nervous crisis.

E2 had an unclouded childhood but emerged into adulthood
                                            inclined to nervous crisis.

E1 led a life of sexual irregularity in the eyes of right-thinking people.

E2 led a life of sexual irregularity in the eyes of right-thinking people.

E1 imagined herself to be in financial difficulties.

E2 knew herself to be in financial difficulties.

E1 committed suicide by swallowing prussic acid.

E2 committed suicide by swallowing arsenic.

E1 was Eleanor Marx.

E2 was Emma Bovary.

The first English translation of *Madame Bovary* to be published was by Eleanor Marx.

Discuss.

Psychoanalysis

Speculate on the significance of this dream, noted down by Flaubert at Lamalgue in 1845: 'I dreamed that I was out walking with my mother in a great forest filled with monkeys. The further we walked, the more of them there were. They were laughing and leaping about in the branches of the trees. There were more and more of them; they got bigger and bigger; they were getting in our way. They kept looking at me, and I became frightened. They surrounded us in a big circle: one of them wanted to stroke me, and took my hand. I shot him in the shoulder with my rifle, and made him bleed; he started howling horribly. Then my mother said to me: "Why did you injure him, he's your friend. What's he done to you? Can't you see that he loves you? And that he looks just like you!" The monkey was looking at me. I felt my soul being torn apart and I woke up . . . feeling as if I was at one with the animals, and fraternising with them in a tender, pantheistic communion.'

Philately

Gustave Flaubert appeared on a French stamp (denomination 8F + 2F) in 1952. It is an indifferent portrait 'after E. Giraud' in which the novelist — slightly Chinese in physiognomy — has been uncharacteristically awarded a modern shirt-collar and tie. The stamp is the lowest denomination in a series issued in aid of the National Relief Fund: the higher denominations celebrate (in ascending order) Manet, Saint-Saëns, Poincaré, Haussmann and Thiers.

Ronsard was the first French writer to appear on a stamp. Victor Hugo figured on three separate stamps between 1933 and 1936, once in a series issued in aid of the Unemployed Intellectuals' Relief Fund. Anatole France's portrait helped this charity in 1937; Balzac's in 1939. Daudet's mill got on a stamp in 1936. Pétainist France celebrated Frédéric Mistral (1941) and Stendhal (1942). Saint-Exupéry, Lamartine and Châteaubriand appeared in 1948; Baudelaire, Verlaine and Rimbaud in the decadent rush of 1951. The latter year also brought stamp-collectors Alfred de Musset, who had succeeded Flaubert in Louise Colet's bed, but now preceded him by one year on to the public envelope.

a) Should we feel slighted on Flaubert's behalf? And if so, should we feel more, or less, slighted on behalf of Michelet (1953), Nerval

(1955), George Sand (1957), Vigny (1963), Proust (1966), Zola (1967), Sainte-Beuve (1969), Mérimée and Dumas *père* (1970), or Gautier (1972)?

b) Estimate the chances of *either* Louis Bouilhet *or* Maxime du Camp *or* Louise Colet appearing on a French stamp.

Phonetics

a) The co-proprietor of the Hôtel du Nil, Cairo, where Flaubert stayed in 1850, was called Bouvaret. The protagonist of his first novel is called Bovary; the co-protagonist of his last novel is called Bouvard. In his play *Le Candidat* there is a Comte de Bouvigny; in his play *Le Château des cœurs* there is a Bouvignard. Is this all deliberate?

b) Flaubert's name was first misprinted by the *Revue de Paris* as Faubert. There was a grocer in the rue Richelieu called Faubet. When *La Presse* reported the trial of *Madame Bovary*, they called its author Foubert. Martine, George Sand's *femme de confiance*, called him Flambart. Camille Rogier, the painter who lived in Beirut, called him Folbert: 'Do you get the subtlety of the joke?' Gustave wrote to his mother. (What is the joke? Presumably a dual-language rendering of the novelist's self-image: Rogier was calling him Crazy Bear.) Bouilhet also started calling him Folbert. In Mantes, where he used to meet Louise, there was a Café Flambert. Is this all coincidence?

c) According to Du Camp, the name Bovary should be pronounced with a short o (as in bother). Should we follow his instruction; and if so, why?

Theatrical History

Assess the technical difficulties involved in implementing the following stage direction (*Le Château des cœurs*, Act VI, scene viii):

The Stock-Pot, the handles of which have been transformed into wings, rises into the air and turns itself over, and while it increases in size so that it appears to hover over the whole town, the vegetables — carrots, turnips and leeks — that come out of it, remain suspended in the air and turn into luminous constellations.

History (with Astrology)

Consider the following predictions of Gustave Flaubert:

a) (1850) 'It seems to me almost impossible that before very long England won't take control of Egypt. Aden is already full of her troops. It couldn't be easier: just across Suez, and one fine morning Cairo will be full of redcoats. The news will reach France a couple of weeks later and we'll all be very surprised! Remember my prediction.'

b) (1852) 'As humanity perfects itself, man becomes degraded. When everything is reduced to the mere counter-balancing of economic interests, what room will there be for virtue? When Nature has been so subjugated that she has lost all her original forms, where will that leave the plastic arts? And so on. In the meantime, things are going to get very murky.'

c) (1870, on the outbreak of the Franco-Prussian war) 'It will mean the return of racial conflicts. Before a century has passed we'll see millions of men killed in a single go. The East against the West, the old world against the new. Why not?'

d) (1850) 'From time to time, I open a newspaper. Things seem to be proceeding at a dizzy rate. We are dancing not on the edge of a volcano, but on the wooden seat of a latrine, and it seems to me more than a touch rotten. Soon society will go plummeting down and drown in nineteen centuries of shit. There'll be quite a lot of shouting.'

e) (1871) 'The Internationals are the Jesuits of the future.'

15

And the Parrot . . .

And the parrot? Well, it took me almost two years to solve the Case of the Stuffed Parrot. The letters I had written after first returning from Rouen produced nothing useful; some of them weren't even answered. Anyone would have thought I was a crank, a senile amateur scholar hooked on trivia and pathetically trying to make a name for himself. Whereas in fact the young are much crankier than the old — far more egotistical, self-destructive and even plain bloody odd. It's just that they get a more indulgent press. When someone of eighty, or seventy, or fifty-four commits suicide, it's called softening of the brain, post-menopausal depression, or a final swipe of mean vanity designed to make others feel guilty. When someone of twenty commits suicide, it's called a high-minded refusal to accept the paltry terms on which life is offered, an act not just of courage but of moral and social revolt. Living? The old can do that for us. Pure crankery, of course. I speak as a doctor.

And while we're on the subject. I should say that the notion of Flaubert killing himself is pure crankery as well. The crankery of a single man: a Rouennais called Edmond Ledoux. This fantasist crops up twice in Flaubert's biography; each time all he does is spread gossip. His first unwelcome utterance is the assertion that Flaubert actually became engaged to Juliet Herbert. Ledoux claimed to have seen a copy of *La Tentation de saint Antoine* inscribed by Gustave to

Juliet with the words '*A ma fiancée*'. Odd that he saw it in Rouen, rather than in London, where Juliet lived. Odd that nobody else ever saw this copy. Odd that it hasn't survived. Odd that Flaubert never mentioned such an engagement. Odd that the act would run diametrically counter to what he believed in.

Odd, too, that Ledoux's other slanderous assertion — of suicide — also runs counter to the writer's deepest beliefs. Listen to him. 'Let us have the modesty of wounded animals, who withdraw into a corner and remain silent. The world is full of people who bellow against Providence. One must, if only on the score of good manners, avoid behaving like them.' And again, that quotation which roosts in my head: 'People like us must have the religion of despair. By dint of saying "That is so! That is so!" and of gazing down into the black pit at one's feet, one remains calm.'

Those are not the words of a suicide. They are the words of a man whose stoicism runs as deep as his pessimism. Wounded animals don't kill themselves. And if you understand that gazing down into the black pit engenders calm, then you don't jump into it. Perhaps this was Ellen's weakness: an inability to gaze into the black pit. She could only squint at it, repeatedly. One glance would make her despair, and despair would make her seek distraction. Some outgaze the black pit; others ignore it; those who keep glancing at it become obsessed. She chose the exact dosage: the only occasion when being a doctor's wife seemed to help her.

Ledoux's account of the suicide goes like this: Flaubert *hanged himself in his bath*. I suppose it's more plausible than saying that he electrocuted himself with sleeping pills; but really ... What happened was this. Flaubert got up, took a hot bath, had an apoplectic fit, and stumbled to a sofa in his study; there he was found expiring by the doctor who later issued the death certificate. That's what happened. End of story. Flaubert's earliest biographer talked to the doctor concerned and that's that. Ledoux's version requires the following chain of events: Flaubert got into his hot bath, hanged himself in some as yet unexplained fashion, then climbed out, hid the rope, staggered to his study, collapsed on the sofa and, when the doctor arrived, managed to die while feigning the symptoms of an apoplectic fit. Really, it's too ridiculous.

No smoke without fire, they say. I'm afraid there can be. Edmond Ledoux is a prime example of spontaneous smoke. Who was he, anyway, this Ledoux? Nobody seems to know. He wasn't an authority on anything. He's a complete nonentity. He only exists as the teller of two lies. Perhaps someone in the Flaubert family once did him harm (did Achille fail to cure his bunion?) and this is his effective revenge. Because it means that few books on Flaubert can end without a discussion − always followed by a dismissal − of the suicide claim. As you see, it's happened all over again here. Another long digression whose tone of moral indignation is probably counter-productive. And I intended writing about the parrots. At least Ledoux didn't have a theory about them.

But I have. Not just a theory, either. As I say, it took me a good two years. No, that's boastful: what I really mean is that two years elapsed between the question arising and dissolving. One of the snobbier academics to whom I wrote even suggested that the matter wasn't really of any interest at all. Well, I suppose he has to guard his territory. Someone, however, gave me the name of M. Lucien Andrieu.

I decided not to write to him; after all, my letters so far hadn't proved very successful. Instead, I made a summer trip to Rouen, in August 1982. I stayed at the Grand Hôtel du Nord, abutting the Gros Horloge. In the corner of my room, running from ceiling to floor, was a soil-pipe, inefficiently boxed-in, which roared at me every five minutes or so, and appeared to carry the waste of the entire hotel. After dinner I lay on my bed listening to the sporadic bursts of Gallic evacuation. Then the Gros Horloge struck the hour with a loud and tinny closeness, as if it were inside my wardrobe. I wondered what the chances of sleep might be.

My apprehension was misconceived. After ten o'clock, the soil-pipe went quiet; and so did the Gros Horloge. It may be a tourist attraction in the daytime, but Rouen thoughtfully disconnects its chimes when visitors are trying to sleep. I lay in bed on my back with the lights out and thought about Flaubert's parrot: to Félicité, it was a grotesque but logical version of the Holy Ghost; to me, a fluttering,

182

elusive emblem of the writer's voice. When Félicité lay in bed dying, the parrot came back to her, in magnified form, and welcomed her into Heaven. As I teetered off towards sleep, I wondered what my dreams might be.

They weren't about parrots. I had my railway dream instead. Changing trains at Birmingham, some time during the war. The distant guard's van at the end of the platform, pulling out. My suitcase rubbing at my calf. The blacked-out train; the station dimly lit. A timetable I couldn't read, a blur of figures. No hope anywhere; no more trains; desolation, darkness.

You'd think such a dream would realise when it had made its point? But dreams have no sense of how they're going down with the dreamer, any more than they have a sense of delicacy. The station dream — which I get every three months or so — simply repeats itself, a loop of film endlessly rerunning, until I wake up heavy-chested and depressed. I awoke that morning to the twin sounds of time and shit: the Gros Horloge and my corner soil-pipe. Time and shit: was Gustave laughing?

At the Hôtel-Dieu the same gaunt, white-coated *gardien* showed me round again. In the medical section of the museum, I noticed something I had missed before: a do-it-yourself enema pump. As hated by Gustave Flaubert: 'Railways, poisons, enema pumps, cream tarts ... ' It consisted of a narrow wooden stool, a hollow spike and a vertical handle. You sat astride the stool, worked your way on to the spike, and then pumped yourself full of water. Well, at least it would give you privacy. The *gardien* and I had a conspiratorial laugh; I told him I was a doctor. He smiled and went to fetch something sure to interest me.

He returned with a large cardboard shoebox containing two preserved human heads. The skin was still intact, though age had turned it brown: as brown as an old jar of redcurrant jam, perhaps. Most of the teeth were in place, but the eyes and hair had not survived. One of the heads had been re-equipped with a coarse black wig and a pair of glass eyes (what colour were they? I can't remember; but less complicated, I'm sure, than the eyes of Emma Bovary). This attempt to make the head more realistic had the opposite effect: it looked like a child's horror mask, a trick-or-treat face from a joke-shop window.

The *gardien* explained that the heads were the work of Jean-Baptiste Laumonier, predecessor of Achille-Cléophas Flaubert at the hospital. Laumonier was looking for new methods of preserving corpses; and the city had allowed him to experiment with the heads of executed criminals. An incident from Gustave's childhood came back to me. Once, out on a walk with his Oncle Parain at the age of six, he had passed a guillotine which had just been used: the cobbles were bright with blood. I mentioned this hopefully; but the *gardien* shook his head. It would have been a nice coincidence, but the dates were incompatible. Laumonier had died in 1818; besides, the two specimens in the shoebox had not in fact been guillotined. I was shown the deep creases just below the jaw where the hangman's noose had once tightened. When Maupassant saw Flaubert's body at Croisset, the neck was dark and swollen. This happens with apoplexy. It's not a sign that someone had hanged himself in the bath.

We continued through the museum until we reached the room containing the parrot. I took out my Polaroid camera, and was allowed to photograph it. As I held the developing print under my armpit, the *gardien* pointed out the Xeroxed letter I had noticed on my first visit. Flaubert to Mme Brainne, July 28th, 1876: 'Do you know what I've had on my table in front of me for the last three weeks? A stuffed parrot. It sits there on sentry duty. The sight of it is beginning to irritate me. But I keep it there so that I can fill my head with the idea of parrothood. Because at the moment I'm writing about the love between an old girl and a parrot.'

'That's the real one,' said the *gardien*, tapping the glass dome in front of us. 'That's the real one.'

'And the other?'

'The other is an impostor.'

'How can you be sure?'

'It's simple. This one comes from the Museum of Rouen.' He pointed to a round stamp on the end of the perch, then drew my attention to a photocopied entry from the Museum register. It recorded a batch of loans to Flaubert. Most of the entries were in some museum shorthand which I couldn't decipher, but the loan of the Amazonian parrot was clearly comprehensible. A series of ticks in the final column of the register showed that Flaubert had returned every item lent to him. Including the parrot.

I felt vaguely disappointed. I had always sentimentally assumed – without proper reason – that the parrot had been found among the writer's effects after his death (this explained, no doubt, why I had secretly been favouring the Croisset bird). Of course the photocopy didn't prove anything, except that Flaubert had borrowed *a* parrot from the Museum, and that he'd returned it. The Museum stamp was a bit trickier, but not conclusive . . .

'Ours is the real one,' the *gardien* repeated unnecessarily as he showed me out. It seemed as if our roles had been reversed: he needed the reassurance, not me.

'I'm sure you're right.'

But I wasn't. I drove to Croisset and photographed the other parrot. It too sported a Museum stamp. I agreed with the *gardienne* that her parrot was clearly authentic, and that the Hôtel-Dieu bird was definitely an impostor.

After lunch I went to the Cimetière Monumental. 'Hatred of the bourgeois is the beginning of all virtue,' wrote Flaubert; yet he is buried amongst the grandest families of Rouen. During one of his trips to London he visited Highgate Cemetery and found it far too neat: 'These people seem to have died with white gloves on.' At the Cimetière Monumental they wear tails and full decorations, and have been buried with their horses, dogs and English governesses.

Gustave's grave is small and unpretentious; in these surroundings, however, the effect is not to make him look an artist, an anti-bourgeois, but rather to make him look an unsuccessful bourgeois. I leaned against the railings which fence off the family plot – even in death you can own a freehold – and took out my copy of *Un cœur simple*. The description Flaubert gives of Félicité's parrot at the start of chapter four is very brief: 'He was called Loulou. His body was green, the ends of his wings pink, his forehead blue, and his throat golden.' I compared my two photographs. Both parrots had green bodies; both had pink wing-tips (there was more pink in the

Hôtel-Dieu version). But the blue forehead and the golden throat: there was no doubting that they belonged to the parrot at the Hôtel-Dieu. The Croisset parrot had it completely back to front: a golden forehead and bluish-green throat.

That seemed to be it, really. All the same, I rang M. Lucien Andrieu and explained my interests in a general way. He invited me to call the next day. As he gave me the address — rue de Lourdines — I imagined the house he was speaking from, the solid, bourgeois house of a Flaubert scholar. The mansard roof pierced with an *oeil-de-boeuf*; the pinkish brick, the Second Empire trimmings; inside, cool seriousness, glass-fronted bookcases, waxed boards and parchment lampshades; I breathed a male, clubby smell.

My briefly-constructed house was an impostor, a dream, a fiction. The real house of the Flaubert scholar was across the river in south Rouen, a run-down area where small industries squat among rows of red-brick terrace houses. Lorries look too big for the streets; there are few shops, and almost as many bars; one was offering *tête de veau* as its *plat du jour*. Just before you get to the rue de Lourdines there is a signpost to the Rouen abattoir.

Monsieur Andrieu was waiting for me on his doorstep. He was a small, elderly man wearing a tweed jacket, tweed carpet slippers and a tweed trilby. There were three ranks of coloured silk in his lapel. He took off his hat to shake hands, then replaced it; his head, he explained, was rather *fragile* in the summer. He was to keep his tweed hat on all the time we were in the house. Some people might have thought this a little cranky, but I didn't. I speak as a doctor.

He was seventy-seven, he informed me, the secretary and oldest surviving member of the Société des Amis de Flaubert. We sat on either side of a table in a front room whose walls were crowded with bric-à-brac: commemorative plates, Flaubert medallions, a painting of the Gros Horloge which M. Andrieu had done himself. It was small and crowded, curious and personal: like a neater version of Félicité's room, or of Flaubert's pavilion. He pointed out a cartoon portrait of himself, drawn by a friend; it showed him as a gunslinger with a large bottle of calvados protruding from his hip pocket. I should have asked the reason for such a ferocious characterisation of my mild and genial host; but I didn't. Instead, I took out my copy of Enid Starkie's *Flaubert: the Making of a Master* and showed him the frontispiece.

'C'est Flaubert, ça?' I asked, just for a final confirmation.

He chuckled.

'C'est Louis Bouilhet. Oui, oui, c'est Bouilhet.' It was clearly not the first time he had been asked. I checked one or two more details with him, and then mentioned the parrots.

'Ah, the parrots. There are two of them.'

'Yes. Do you know which is the true one and which is the impostor?'

He chuckled again.

'They set up the museum at Croisset in 1905,' he replied. 'The year of my birth. Naturally, I was not there. They gathered together what material they could find — well, you've seen it for yourself.' I nodded. 'There wasn't much. Many things had been dispersed. But the curator decided that there was one thing they could have, and that was Flaubert's parrot. Loulou. So they went to the Museum of Natural History and said, Can we please have Flaubert's parrot back. We want it for the pavilion. And the Museum said, Of course, come with us.'

Monsieur Andrieu had told this story before; he knew its pauses.

'So, they took the curator to where they kept the reserve collection. You want a parrot? they said. Then we go to the section of the birds. They opened the door, and they saw in front of them . . . fifty parrots. *Une cinquantaine de perroquets*!

'What did they do? They did the logical thing, the intelligent thing. They came back with a copy of *Un cœur simple*, and they read to themselves Flaubert's description of Loulou.' Just as I had done the day before. 'And then they chose the parrot which looked most like his description.

'Forty years later, after the last war, they started making the collection at the Hôtel-Dieu. They in their turn went back to the Museum and said, Please can we have Flaubert's parrot. Of course, said the Museum, take your pick, but make sure you get the right one. So they too consulted *Un cœur simple*, and chose the parrot which most resembled Flaubert's description. And that's how there are two parrots.'

'So the pavilion at Croisset, which had the first choice, must have the true parrot?'

M. Andrieu looked non-committal. He pushed his tweed trilby slightly further back on his head. I took out my photographs. 'But if so, what about this?' I quoted the familiar description of the parrot, and pointed to the non-conforming forehead and breast of the Croisset version. Why should the parrot chosen second look more like the one in the book than the parrot chosen first?

'Well. You have to remember two things. One, Flaubert was an artist. He was a writer of the imagination. And he would alter a fact for the sake of a cadence; he was like that. Just because he borrowed a parrot, why should he describe it as it was? Why shouldn't he change the colours round if it sounded better?

'Secondly, Flaubert returned his parrot to the Museum after he'd finished writing the story. That was in 1876. The pavilion was not set up until thirty years later. Stuffed animals get the moth, you know. They fall apart. Félicité's did, after all, didn't it? The stuffing came out of it.'

'Yes.'

'And perhaps they change colour with time. Of course, I am not an expert in the stuffing of animals.'

'So you mean either of them could be the real one? Or, quite possibly, neither?'

He spread his hands slowly on the table, in a conjuror's calming gesture. I had a final question.

'Are there still all those parrots left at the Museum? All fifty of them?'

'I don't know. I don't think so. You have to know that in the Twenties and Thirties, when I was young, there was a great fashion for stuffed animals and birds. People had them in their sitting-rooms. They thought they were pretty. So, a lot of museums sold off parts of their collections which they didn't need. Why should they hold on to fifty Amazonian parrots? They would only decay. I don't know how many they have now. I should think the Museum got rid of most of them.'

We shook hands. On the doorstep M. Andrieu raised his hat to me, briefly uncovering his fragile head to the August sun. I felt pleased and disappointed at the same time. It was an answer and not an answer; it was an ending, and not an ending. As with Félicité's final heartbeats, the story was dying away 'like a fountain running dry, like an echo disappearing'. Well, perhaps that's as it should be.

It was time to pay farewell. Like a conscientious doctor, I made the rounds of Flaubert's three statues. What shape was he in? At Trouville his moustache still needs repair; though the patching on his thigh now looks less conspicuous. At Barentin, his left leg is beginning to split, there is a hole in the corner of his jacket, and a mossy discoloration spots his upper body; I stared at the greenish marks on his chest, half-closed my eyes, and tried to turn him into a Carthaginian interpreter. At Rouen, in the place des Carmes, he is structurally sound, confident in his alloy of 93 per cent copper and 7 per cent tin; but he still continues to streak. Each year he seems to cry a couple more cupreous tears, which brightly vein his neck. This isn't inappropriate: Flaubert was always a great weeper. The tears continue on down his body, giving him a fancy waistcoat and putting thin side-stripes on his legs, as if he were wearing dress-trousers. This too isn't inappropriate: it's a reminder that he enjoyed salon life as well as his Croisset retreat.

A few hundred yards north, at the Museum of Natural History, they took me upstairs. This was a surprise: I'd assumed that reserve collections were always held in cellars. Nowadays they probably have leisure centres down there instead: cafeterias and wall-charts and video-games and everything to make learning easy. Why are they so keen to turn learning into a game? They love to make it childish, even for adults. Especially for adults.

It was a small room, perhaps eight feet by ten, with windows on the right and shelves running away to the left. Despite a few ceiling lights, it remained quite dark, this burial vault on the top floor. Though it wasn't, I suppose, altogether a tomb: some of these creatures would be taken out again into the daylight, and allowed to replace moth-eaten or unfashionable colleagues. So it was an ambivalent room, half-morgue and half-purgatory. It had an uncertain smell, too: somewhere between a surgery and a hardware shop.

Everywhere I looked there were birds. Shelf after shelf of birds, each one covered in a sprinkling of white pesticide. I was directed to the third aisle. I pushed carefully between the shelves and then looked up at a slight angle. There, standing in a line, were the Amazonian parrots. Of the original fifty only three remained. Any gaudiness in their colouring had been dimmed by the dusting of pesticide which lay over them. They gazed at me like three quizzical, sharp-eyed, dandruff-ridden, dishonourable old men. They did look — I had to admit it — a little cranky. I stared at them for a minute or so, and then dodged away.

Perhaps it was one of them.